A PLACE OF WHISPERS

by
Gil Jackman

authorHOUSE®

AuthorHouse™ UK Ltd.
500 Avebury Boulevard
Central Milton Keynes, MK9 2BE
www.authorhouse.co.uk
Phone: 08001974150

First published by AuthorHouse   02/24/2011

ISBN: 978-1-4567-7617-6 (sc)

CHAPTER ONE

OLD MEN DREAM.

They rarely dream the youthful uncertainties of the future, or the adults' unease of the present. When old men dream their memories assist, for to them the present and the future mean nought. They might prefer their fonder memories, but the privilege of age does not always bring what is desired.

For a few years now Joseph had been travelling further back in his mind during dream-time, a happening which the white mind-doctors would call regression. There was a time when Joseph found it difficult to remember past a certain age and date, yet now he could resurrect much of his earlier life; the men and women he had known, now mere shades in the mortal world he inhabited still.

Most of all he dreamed of his childhood in the shadow of *uKhahlamba*, the Barrier of Uplifted Spears. The Dutchmen gave it the name Drakensberg, Dragon Mountains, and when they tried to speak in the Bantu tongue they said 'Quathlamba', but they were wrong.

He dreamed of his first hunt, the painful initiation to become a man, marriage to his first and only wife, who would be his first love always. His first child, and the unbounded joy that it was male; and the tragedy that followed fulfilment.

Only when morning came, returning him from the shadow-lands, did the uncertainties of youth, and the unease of their fathers, come back. For even old men have their worries and the stark light of day did not respect the oblivion of night. With the dawn came the realities of his situation.

His life of the past thirty years was over, swept away like the drought wind drives the dust of shrivelled mealies, as though they had never existed. Like a horse that has given long and faithful service, he too would be put out to grass. It was the way of the Whites.

Yet unlike the horse, Joseph was not destined to remain in familiar pastures.

'He will get what my father wanted him to have, of course,' Joseph heard the young *baas* say. 'But we can't keep him on much longer. The man is obviously senile and any day now he'll hurt himself, or God forbid, one of the children.'

His wife did not reply. If she did she would find herself defending the old man, insisting that he stay on. Which in turn would upset the young *baas*, for he did not like to be argued with. Especially by his woman.

So when the little *baas* spoke it came as a surprise to everyone. His mother and two sisters stared, and his father frowned in a way that the old servant knew well. As a teenager that frown would appear when he could not get his own way, and it usually presaged a tantrum.

Joseph crept quietly from the dining room, back to his kitchen. He could still hear through the hatch, and did not have to be present when the young *baas* began shouting.

He would not be missed, for the young *baas* spoke about him as though he was not there.

'What did you say, young man?' His voice was ominously quiet, and from the next room Joseph could feel his anger like a palpable thing.

'I asked w...why J...Joseph has t...to g...go. He's n...not s... senile, f...father, and h...he b...belongs here,' the boy replied. The young *baas* had never allowed his children to call him anything but father. Paternal or maternal diminutives were forbidden.

'Nonsense,' his father said coldly. 'He drops things all the time, and he's always mislaying something. His cooking has become terrible. That's senility, Michael. Do you still maintain that he belongs here?'

'Y...yes, f...father,' the boy stammered bravely. 'It's h...his eyesight t...that is the t...trouble. It's b...bad, and h...he m... might need n...new glasses.'

'He has a perfectly good pair of glasses,' the young *baas* snapped. 'I remember my father buying them for him.'

'It was a long time ago, dear,' the missus said hesitantly. 'Perhaps they should be replaced by a stronger pair.'

'Rubbish,' the old man could picture the young *baas* waving his hand in a dismissive gesture. 'I'll get some quotes next week and they can begin building. A little hut in *kwaZulu* is all he wants, and with the pension fund father set up he'll have all he needs for the rest of his life.'

Wants...needs...what did they know of his wants and needs?

A little hut in *kwaZulu*. The old man sat at the kitchen table and shook his head. It was true he had come from *kwaZulu*, so many years before, but it was not where he wanted his bones to rest.

His home was not the land of the Zulu. Joseph was Ngwane, and *uKhahlamba* would always be his home.

Aware of the presence of another, the old man looked up.

Into the sad eyes of the little *baas*. Once the boy's father had been little *baas*, then young *baas* to distinguish him from the master.

'I'm very sorry, Joseph,' the boy said, and the old man knew it was so. When they spoke together it was a mixture of English and Zulu, their own version of *Fanagalo*, the bastard language of the mines that was now called 'kitchen Zulu' by the Whites.

When he spoke to the old man, the boy never stammered, a peculiarity that would make Joseph smile sadly to himself.

'I too am sorry,' the servant said softly. 'I too, little *baas*.'

'I'm not your little *baas*, Joseph,' the boy said with a dignity that an *induna* would have envied. 'I am your friend.'

The old man had smiled through his sadness, for it was true. The boy WAS his friend.

His ONLY friend.

Joseph was not certain how old he was, for he had no idea of the year when he was born. His mother had died when he was a baby, and his father's new wives had taken him into their *rondavels* and raised him. He was somewhere in his early twenties when his wife died of fever. Unable to remain where the memories were too much to bear, he began the travels which would last until he arrived in the city on the coast of Natal.

He was approaching his middle years when he began knocking on many doors, seeking employment. By now he spoke Afrikaans and English well, but did not show it for many Whites were resentful and suspicious of 'clever *kaffirs*'. When he arrived at the house on the Berea the wind of luck touched him as it passed, for the gardener was old and they took Joseph on.

First he was assistant to the old gardener, and when he retired Joseph took over. After a while the missus took him out of the garden and into the house, and there he had remained. Until now.

When the old missus died Joseph and the *baas* had fallen into an easy routine which suited them both. At first there had been Gladys the cook, then she had been retired to her family farm in *kwaZulu* where the old *baas* built a small house for her. Joseph had learned from her, and became both cook and houseboy. A young Zulu, Willie, did the garden and all the heavy work about the house.

Joseph and Willie had a *kya* each behind the house, and the three men lived together quietly and amicably. Each man knew his role in the household. Willie deferred to the old cook, and Joseph in his turn deferred to the *baas*.

The old *baas*, Michael's grandfather, never fully recovered from the loss of his adored wife. She had been ill for many years, bedridden for her last eight, yet she had never lost her humour and good nature. It was always a pleasure for Joseph to take her meals into her, for she would make him sit by her bed and they would talk whilst she ate. At first the *baas* frowned upon this, but she insisted she enjoyed the company and their talk of far places, and he relented. Only she was aware of the black man's usage of English, and his discerning and enquiring mind.

After the young *baas* had married and left home, the old *baas* would take his evening meal with the missus in her room. When she finally went to her rest, the house had taken on a loneliness that the two older men both felt deeply.

In an attempt to get through the long evenings, the old *baas* bought a television set, although he'd been critical for years, regarding them as mindless pleasure devices. He was an abstemious man, and would take two whiskies and sodas before dinner and no more after.

The lounge was big with a door at one end leading to the dining-room, facing a passage which led to the front door with bedrooms off to either side. Once there had been two small dogs, and a wrought-iron railing had been constructed to keep them in the lounge, extending the passage along to the dining-room door.

At night Gladys, Joseph and Willie would sit on chairs behind the railing, watching television in the remote company of the old *baas*. The programmes were in English or Afrikaans, with the occasional Zulu news report, and between much whispering the combined linguistics of the servants were able to sort out plots and events.

Most nights Gladys would begin to doze, then drift off to her *kya*. She would soon be followed by Willie, who, after the novelty of the colour and the action wore off, found it hard to follow all but the simplest of stories. Then the old *baas* and Joseph would talk together. Sometimes the old *baas* would invite Joseph to join him in a nightcap, and over a glass of port or brandy they would discuss many things, long into the night.

Each on their own side of the wrought-iron gate. An absurdity perhaps, but both old men felt comfortable that way, with the distinction between master and servant still maintained.

Before Michael's grandfather died, he and the old Ngwane had become friends. In a way he was the only real friend the ex-banker had. He had acquaintances and colleagues of course, but they were just that. Acquaintances and colleagues - not friends.

His wife had been the one for friends. In their younger days, the vibrant English beauty and the tall shy South African had been part of the Durban social scene. With her by his side, incredibly, he seemed to fit in. It was the contrast, their friends said. In a nice way of course. Her fragility against his solidness; her gaiety and his quiet seriousness; her fondness for, and acceptance of, life...and his denial.

That she should have been the one struck down with an incurable illness was a travesty of fate that even he had to question. From the day she was confined to her bed until the day she died, he never attended church.

Only her dying wish drew him back to his faith, before it was his turn to join her.

In the way of the warrior, Joseph made his mind up quickly, and he smiled wistfully as the thought came unbidden into his head. For it was a long time since he had considered himself a warrior.

Before the sun chased the moon away, he had risen and begun to prepare himself for his journey. Ignoring the two battered cases, he took the big leather bag from beneath his cot. He packed it carefully with things from the present, and much of long ago.

From hooks on the wall he took his weapons; fighting sticks and short stabbing spears. A loose brick in the wall of the *kya* produced a bundle of money, notes to the value of nearly R1000, carefully saved from his wages. The bulk went to the village in the valleys of the Mnweni, where the waters of the Umlambonja raced from Cathedral Peak, gathering the cold fast-flowing mountain streams to provide irrigation for the maize crops of the Amangwane.

The village he had not seen in many long years, the place of his fondest dreams, and in those dreams there was little noise. It was his Place of Whispers, for it was said amongst his people that if there was a place on the earth that you wished to return, you must not speak its name aloud. It must be only whispered, for the mischievous Gods, whose task it was to thwart the desires of men, would make sure that you never saw that place again in this lifetime.

It was with a sad heart that the old man looked at the house from the back gate, his knapsack slung over his stooped shoulders. So many years. Years in which he had come to know the Whites in some small measure. The gentleness of the old missus, and that same kindness that was in the young one. The final mellowing of the old *baas*, and their quiet times together.

Then his death, and the young *baas* and his family moving in.

The young *baas* expected him to cook for them all again, but Joseph found it hard to see close up these days. When first he had his glasses he'd been able to read the newspapers, like the old missus had taught him, and he'd borrowed many books from the library shelves in the lounge. Now the print was blurred and he could make out very little.

There had been many months of peace and quiet for Joseph and Willie before the family came. It was used as a holiday home only when the young *baas* worked in Pietermaritzburg, and it was kept spotless with no-one to mess it up. Each night the two servants would eat their *putu*, *samp* and meat, and watch the television.

Still behind the railing, of course, for that was how the old black man insisted it must be, to the puzzlement of the younger.

The peaceful life had ended with the permanence of the young *baas* and his family. If the young missus tried to help Joseph in the kitchen her husband would scold her, saying it was what they paid the servants for. The little *baas* was not a good scholar, and he too was always close to the wrath of his father.

When he joined the school climbing club, and showed a keen interest in the sport, his father had done his best to deter him. The traditional sports of cricket and rugby were the only real activities to pursue as far as he was concerned, and the rest were a waste of time. Even then, academic subjects came first.

Each school holiday was the same. The boy would ask diffidently if he could accompany the club on a climbing trip to the Drakensberg, and each time the young *baas's* answer was firm and unyielding. Not until his grades improved, his father would say, secure in the knowledge that they never would be good enough. For him.

One day Joseph opened the door to the boy's science teacher, who was also the climbing instructor, and he couldn't help overhearing the conversation with the young *baas*. Michael was an excellent climber, the teacher said, and if there was a problem about cost the school had funds which could be used to assist his inclusion on a trip.

The young *baas* had been furious at the presumption. He could afford a dozen trips if necessary, he snapped, but Michael would be going into Standard 5 next term, and his holidays would be spent attending remedial classes in mathematics and English.

Feeling sorrow for his young friend, as well as for himself, the old man hefted his burden and turned to begin his lonely trek to the west.

To *uKhahlamba*, and his Place of Whispers.

'You would leave without saying good-bye, Joseph?'

The old man's head turned around in surprise. The first few rays of dawn were crawling across the sky, yet they were not needed. By the street light near the gate he could see the little *baas* quite plainly.

'I have enough sadness in my heart without that too, little *baas*,' Joseph said softly.

'Perhaps if you had, the sadness would not have been so bad,' the boy smiled. 'I'm coming with you.'

'No, you cannot...' the old man was suddenly frightened. No one would look for him alone, in fact the young *baas* would be pleased that he had rid himself of the old servant without the cost of a house in *kwaZulu* and his small pension. But with the little *baas* missing, they would search everywhere...

'I'm coming, Joseph,' the tones were firm, without hint of stammer. 'Someone must look after you. I know your eyes are bad, and you will be robbed, or cheated. Besides, I have always wanted to go to the Drakensberg. That's where you're going, isn't it?'

Joseph had often talked, in the lowest of voices of course, about his village in uKhahlamba, his boyhood games and his hunts as a warrior. Michael's friends in the climbing club had also told him about it, of the fantastic peaks and rock formations, and how wonderful it was to climb there.

'I cannot stop you, little *baas*,' the old man held his hands out from his sides in a gesture of defeat. 'But I wish you would not.'

'Your objection is duly noted, sir,' grinned the boy, whose verbal vocabulary was far better than his written, and he mounted the last few steps to street level. He was dressed in warm bush-clothes and stout *velkskoens,* and carried a hiking pack on his wiry shoulders. Already the aspect of a frightened buck had dropped from him, and to the older man he looked confident and happy for once.

With an exaggerated sigh that was filled with pleasure, he beckoned to the young boy and they began the long, but no longer lonely, journey inland.

Joseph led the way down the hill to the Greyville racecourse, and he told Michael they would have to walk around, for they needed to be on the other side. The boy grinned and showed him where a loose plank could be lifted out of the fence. They crossed the track, ducking under the white rails, and strolled over the Royal Durban Golf Course in the centre.

They re-crossed the track and again Michael knew a way through the fence. Pretending to be shocked by his knowledge, but appreciative, the old man followed him through. It was now his turn to take over, and they walked on to a roundabout some two kilometres from the racecourse. The sun had appeared in its rightful place in the heavens, but not yet in all its glory.

'There is one waiting, little *baas*,' Joseph grinned, showing teeth that a man half his age would have been proud of.

'Great,' the boy was delighted. 'I've always wanted to ride in a *kaffir* taxi...I'm sorry, Joseph, I mean a Black taxi.'

'It is the same thing, I think,' the old man smiled, then considered for a moment. 'Did you know that the word *kafir*, with one F, is an Arabic word? Truly, and in that language it is also derisory but not directed at Blacks only, for it means anyone who is an unbeliever of the Koran. Come, this will begin our journey.'

He exchanged a few words in Zulu with the driver, who replied politely in deference to his age.

'It will take us as far as Hammarsdale,' Joseph told Michael. 'Then we must leave the roads and travel across country, for they will be looking for us.'

The taxi was a Kombi van, like all the Black taxis throughout the country. It soon filled up, and the vehicle made its way onto the N3, the western freeway.

'One thing we must get straight,' the boy insisted. The taxi swerved dangerously around a slow-moving lorry, as though trying to keep the unsafe reputation of its kind. 'I am no longer little *baas*. You've left my father's employ, and you are my friend. Therefore you must call me Michael, please.'

'As you say,' the crinkly grey head bowed solemnly. 'Michael.'

The taxi came off the freeway at Hammarsdale and stopped at the garage at the edge of the small town. The driver exchanged a few words with Joseph, who thanked him and the taxi began to load up with passengers for the trip back. Itinerant workers, who lived there and went to Durban each day for work.

'What did the driver say?' the boy asked, as they moved off into the bush. The garage attendants watched them indifferently. They saw many strange things these days, which it paid to ignore.

'He said to leave this area quickly,' the old man muttered. 'It is a bad place. Many murders have happened here.'

Michael remembered seeing something about it on the news. Taxi wars and faction fights, little of it political, but all causing suffering to innocent people.

They followed a well-worn path for a kilometre then suddenly came out before a collection of crudely erected dwellings. Whatever material could be found had been used in their construction. Tin and plastic sheeting, old crates, oil tins beaten flat.

People stared without curiosity as they walked past, although they must have looked an incongruous pair. The old Black wearing his best Sunday suit, shirt buttoned to the neck with no tie. Well polished shoes worn without socks. Accompanied by a young White, dressed for a bush trek.

They did not speak, and Joseph did not acknowledge their presence.

'Who were they?' the boy asked, after they had left the place well behind. It was not like Joseph to ignore people that way.

'They are Xhosa,' he said shortly. 'Come up from the Transkei, their homeland. They squat here on land that is not theirs, and take work from the Zulu.'

'But surely they were pushed into the homelands when they started the land act, or something,' Michael frowned, wishing he'd paid more attention in school to the history of his country.

'Transkei is the land of the Xhosa,' Joseph said. 'It is true they came to Southern Africa before the Zulu, part of the great migration of the tribes from Zimbabwe, and they fought the Hottentot and Bushman. They were the only migratory people who mated with the Hottentots instead of helping to wipe them out, and they have much Hottentot blood. They also absorbed much of the Hottentot and Bushmen languages.'

'That would explain the click sounds they have,' Michael said, very impressed with the old man's knowledge, as well as the command of English that he'd previously kept to himself.

Joseph nodded. They had stopped to rest, and the old man mopped his brow with a large handkerchief, a gift from the old *baas*.

'The Xhosa was a fierce fighter, in the old days. Unlike the Zulu, who likes pointed and edged metal weapons such as spears and axes, the Xhosa prefers blunt objects, like clubs and heavy sticks. They were poor metal workers and their spears were too long and clumsy for hand-to-hand fighting. He scorns a shield, even today, and carries two fighting sticks, where the Zulu will carry a shield and stick.'

He'd taken out an ancient corn-cob pipe and began stuffing it with coarse tobacco.

'The Xhosa are famous for being cheats and thieves, especially cattle thieves, and they like nothing better than to outwit people. But some are good fighters still. One of their best weapons is a blanket.' He saw the disbelief in the boy's face and smiled. 'Yes, Michael. He throws it at his opponent's eyes, at the point of his spear, or entangles his legs in it. Some tie stones or balls of lead into the corners, then swing it in such a way that it strikes their opponent on the head. The Xhosa is cunning, and not to be trusted.'

The boy was silent, thinking of the times he'd heard his father talking politics, of how Mr Mandela had done a reasonably good job of keeping the country from a huge bloodbath. It was a frightening thought if the people Joseph described took over when Mr Mandela resigned or died. At the same time he remembered hearing Xhosa politicians on TV say the same thing about the Zulus. It was all beyond him.

They carried on, Joseph still smoking his foul-smelling pipe, causing Michael to fall back a distance behind him. They left the track after the rest-halt, and the old man seemed to know just where he was going as they struck out across country.

When the boy questioned him on this, he merely shrugged, and the subject was dropped.

They camped an hour before dusk. A small stream of clear water had crossed their path, and Joseph said it was an omen to stop there for the night. A check of their food provided interesting contrasts. Where Joseph had brought rice, mealie meal, *biltong* and cooked meat, Michael had brought tins, packets of biscuits, bread, and even uncooked potatoes. Joseph had an old cooking pot that the young missus had thrown out long ago, and Michael had a frying pan.

The old man refrained from comment or criticism, and lit a fire in a way that amazed the young boy. By the time he returned with more wood, there was a pot of hot tea waiting. The leather bag produced two battered tin mugs.

'I always carry a spare in case I have a visitor,' the old man grinned. 'I did not know that the first visitor would become a fixture.'

The boy grinned back. It was the best cup of tea he'd ever tasted, and he said so.

They dined well, that first night. Most of the potatoes went into the pot, with tins of beans and beef chunks. Joseph picked herbs and leaves, adding them to the stew, and Michael said it was the best stew he'd ever tasted. The old man smiled, and said it was a day of bests and firsts indeed.

While the old man tended the meal, he directed Michael to make a bivouac shelter of thin sticks with a covering of leaves and grasses, beneath which they laid their bedding. The boy had a sleeping bag, and Joseph a blanket, with a thin *duiker* skin to keep the coldness of the ground from his old bones.

They built up the fire and turned in, but it was only 7.30, and despite that it had been the longest day of the boy's young life he found it hard to sleep. The old man too lay wide awake, for beneath his calm demeanour his heart was also bursting with excitement.

'I think your parents will be worrying very much now, Michael,' Joseph said softly, with no reproach or criticism in his voice.

'My mother will,' the boy replied. 'I shouldn't think it would have stopped my father from his Thursday golf game.'

'I think you misjudge your father,' the old man said. 'Do not accept everything at face value, for actions do not always indicate what is in a man's heart. He loves you very much, you know.'

'Perhaps,' Michael sounded doubtful. 'But sometimes I think he'd rather have his golf clubs that me.'

Joseph knew there was no point in pursuing the argument. The boy would have to find out many things for himself, the love of his father being one of them.

Instead he changed the subject.

'Your father plays at the Durban Country Club, yes? Well, I have a good friend there, with who I often visit. His name is Fredo, and he is the head caddy.'

'I think I know him,' Michael sat up. 'A few months ago my father took me there to begin lessons, and Fredo was the man who was to teach me. He was very kind, and very patient with me when I showed I couldn't hit the ball anywhere.'

'I heard about it,' the old man said with amusement. 'Your father was not too pleased about it. I think he knew the Saturday morning lessons were at the same time as your climbing club meetings.'

The boy stared at him and saw the humour on his face, for it does not get dark until late in Africa. 'You knew I kept missing the ball on purpose. I suppose your friend, Fredo, told you.'

'He did say that your heart was not in it, *jong*,' Joseph smiled.

'I think my father planned it that way on purpose,' the boy said hotly. 'He'd do anything to stop me from enjoying myself.'

'No, Michael. He would do anything to stop you from climbing. It is not the same thing, for he worries about you doing it. I have heard he and your mother talking about it many times. Now, I will tell you a tale of my friend Fredo, when he was a young man. Remember, there are lessons to be learned from every story.'

'Great,' the boy cried. 'I love stories.'

THE RIGHT PRICE

The place where Fredo worked was of an age with his grandfather, who was an old man when he died. The Durban Country Club was an institution both to those who had successfully negotiated the uppermost rungs of the social ladder, or who perched precariously at the halfway point. Much as his grandfather had been an institution to his people in their *kraal* up in Zululand.

Membership of the Country Club was mandatory if one professed to be part of that Durban elite, just as membership of the Bowling Club was essential to the White working class of the city.

The main activity of the Country Club was golf. Fredo was a caddy there, having managed to talk himself into a part-time job at thirteen. In six months he'd more than proved his worth and was taken on full-time.

Fredo enjoyed hefting a heavy bag of clubs on his shoulder and trotting along behind his golfer. He'd been a full-time caddy for six years now, and went round the course once or twice a day. Sometimes three times in the summer, and he knew everything there was to know about the game of golf.

Except what it felt like to play.

The club rules were very strict on that point. Caddies did not use the greens under any circumstances.

Fredo was paid nothing by the club, and the set fee as laid down was only R5.50. Most players gave him a R5 note and two R1 coins, with a magnanimous 'keep the change'. At that time the exchange rate for the rand against the English pound was R5.50, though today it is almost R10.

Others would pay not a penny over the set price, and even then they would argue between themselves over who paid. Sometimes, though not often, both players would give him R5 each.

Fredo preferred to caddy for the ladies. For one thing their bags were lighter. The ladies only carried what they used, about five or six clubs at the most. Mr Archibald, one of the worst players, and biggest cheats, made his caddy drag around a bag with fifteen clubs in it, some of which he hadn't used in years.

The ladies were also more appreciative of his value as a caddy, for although he couldn't play himself, his many times over the course had given him a sound knowledge of how to play each hole. His advice was often asked, and taken, by the ladies.

Never the men.

His favourite lady was Miss Goodhew, who called him by his first name and always tipped well.

Wagers were made between players, and a jubilant winner might be inclined to reward his caddy with a nice tip. Occasionally.

During his years at the Country Club, Fredo had noticed several anomalies. The highest bets were between the not-so-wealthy members. The best losers were among the more socially humble, and the most generous tips to the caddies were from the least affluent.

Also, the biggest cheats were the richest.

At first the young Zulu found it hard to believe that such people could do these things. It obviously wasn't for the rewards of the wager, for usually they wouldn't go beyond R2 a hole. It was something else, an elusive thing that the young man could not comprehend.

It could surely not be pride in winning, his honest mind would puzzle, for how could there be pride if cheating was involved in the winning?

Take Mr Frensham-Smith. He was the president of the club and an important man at the Bank. Yet he cheated at every opportunity. He was not one of the best players and would take two, three, or even four shots over the par. Fredo would often count 7 or 8 hits when he caddied for Mr Frensham-Smith.

When he would finally get onto the green, he would call in a loud voice, 'How many IS that, caddy? Four or five?'

And Fredo would reply, 'Four'.

Mr Frensham-Smith would shake his head reluctantly and say modestly, 'I thought it was five myself, but if the caddy says four...'

Fredo was astute enough to know that in the man's mind it was not himself cheating, but his caddy. Of course, there was always a small tip at the end of the game to ease his conscience.

One of the most consistent cheats was Colonel Potbury, an Englishman, who was so blatant that at first the caddy did not realise what he was doing. Rumour had it that he had been a mere subaltern in the British army, seconded to India as acting Major in charge of the native troops. His title derived from the few months he'd spent before Partition as a local colonel.

He could certainly act like a colonel, and was often heard berating the Indian waiters over some imaginary tardiness, and he expected his gin and bitters to be produced instantly when he walked into the clubhouse.

The Colonel used every method to cheat that Fredo had ever seen in his years at the club, and his favourite was the most obvious, yet the easiest to get away with.

Many a time the young caddy had seen the Colonel's ball go into the rough and he'd plodded after him hauling the antique bag of heavy leather. Many golfers had little carts to pull their bags along, but not the Colonel. If his ball was in a particularly bad placement for a good shot, he would pick it up and study it closely.

'Yes, by jove,' he'd say in surprise. 'It IS my ball, after all. Just making sure.'

And he would put it down in a prime position. Once he had been cheeky enough to place it carefully on top of a molehill, at least 30cms above the surrounding scrub. To the astonishment of his opponent, the Colonel's drive from the trees had landed on the green and actually struck the flag.

Fredo's favourite man to caddy for was Mr Strydom. He was not a native of Durban, though this in itself was not held against him. That his father was a plumber and originally from the Transvaal, well, these were another matter to the Country Club members.

His father being successful enough as a plumber to finance his son through university, where he gained an engineering degree with honours, did nothing to obviate his pedigree.

Mr Strydom was also one of the best golfers in the club, and this too did nothing to help. He'd gained admittance to the club under the auspices of Mr Goodhew, the owner of the engineering firm where he worked. Mr Strydom was a research engineer, and Fredo had heard that he was responsible for many new products.

Not that Mr Goodhew treated the cause of his prosperity with the generosity one would have expected. His sole reason for gaining him entry to the Country Club appeared to be to keep Mr Strydom firmly in his place.

That he had taken naturally to the game of golf had not been in Mr Goodhew's reckoning. Nor that he had won the heart of his employer's daughter. On both counts he was doomed to stay forever in Mr Goodhew's bad books, and in the shadow of his favourite, Mr Attwood-Myers, a respectable product of Durban 'old money'.

Mr Attwood-Myers was the best golfer in the Country Club.

He had proved this by winning the Champion's Cup for the past four years. He was also the marketing manager for Mr Goodhew's firm, and destined for a seat on the board. If either of them had any say in the matter he would also be married to Mr Goodhew's daughter at the same time.

'I've even seen Mr Atty cheat at golf,' Fredo told his friend Imran, who was another caddy. Imran was Indian and Fredo considered him very clever. 'But never Mr Strydie.'

The caddies had their own nicknames for the members.

'I too have seen him cheat,' Imran agreed. 'He is very good at it, for the better the player the harder it is for them to be cheating.'

'Why is that?' his friend frowned.

'Why, it is obvious,' Imran replied. 'The good players are going around in about 78 or so, and get their holes close to the par, which is usually 3 or 4. This is consisting of a tee shot and a couple of puttings on the green, and everyone is seeing them. How then can they cheat?'

'I see,' Fredo had caught on. 'It is only when they make a bad shot that they can recover by cheating.'

'Of course, and that is when we caddies can make some good tipping, my friend.'

'It is still wrong,' Fredo insisted. 'I was taught by my grandfather that cheating is not a good thing.'

'I know you are right,' the Indian boy agreed. 'But it is the club members who are doing it, and who are we to give them verbal annoyance about it? WE would be the ones in trouble, Fredo.'

Fredo was forced to agree.

A few weeks later the Durban Country Club held its annual championship. Because it was also the club's centennial, many local businesses had donated money towards a grand prize. Apart from the usual silver cup, there was R100,000 in cash for the winner, and there was much speculation and interest over the event.

None more so than between Mr Strydie and Miss Goody. Fredo was caddying for them as they played a friendly game one Sunday morning, and he could not help but overhear their talk.

'It would be enough for us to get married and live on while I look for another job,' Mr Strydom said. 'I'm fed up of your father making money from pinching my ideas, without even the courtesy of a small bonus. Attwood's in on it too, agrees with everything the old man says. I'd love to open in opposition to them. I could produce stuff better AND cheaper.'

'Oh, I agree, darling,' Miss Goodhew cried. 'I've been thinking about that and we could use the money grandmother left me. With the prize money it would be enough.'

There was a brightness in her eyes, and the watching caddy thought she was the prettiest White girl he'd ever seen. Not that she could compere with his Beauty, of course. She took after her name, and her eyes would shine when he called her his Black Beauty, after a book they'd read in school. In five more years of saving they would have enough to get married and buy their own place.

It did not come as a surprise to anyone that Mr Attwood-Myers reached the final of the tournament. The surprise was his opponent. Mr Strydom had played his heart out, and on one of his games he'd missed the course record by only two points. Part of his success was Miss Goodhew telling him about Fredo's intimate knowledge of the course, and his uncanny instinct for directing the ball.

Of course, this guidance could only be of use if the player was good enough to send the ball where the caddy told him, and Mr Strydom had showed he was.

They were now teeing off for the seventeenth, and Fredo felt very proud of Mr Strydom as he watched him from the edge of the tee. Standing next to him was Imran, who was caddying for Mr Attwood-Myers. There was not much in it. Mr Attwood-Myers was only 2 points behind, but by his attitude it could have been twenty. He complained about everything and poor Imran bore the brunt of his sharp tongue.

He was the first to tee off and his ball drove straight towards the far flag, before suddenly veering to the left and into the stand of sycamores. Cursing to himself, he moved away from the tee, as Mr Strydom called Fredo over and they discussed the drive in low voices.

'What the hell's the chinwag for, Strydom?' Mr Attwood-Myers called irritably. 'What the devil does he know about golf? He's just a caddy. And a Black one at that.'

Voices were raised in agreement from the watching crowd, and Mr Goodhew's was one of the loudest. Mr Strydom glanced over at them and smiled, as he clapped Fredo on the shoulder and winked.

His ball went in line with the tall oak to the right of the flag, but as the young caddy had calculated, the wind that stirred the tops of the trees pushed it. To land 50 yards in front of the green.

'Well done, Fredo,' Mr Strydom grinned at his caddy, and they walked down the centre of the fairway together, side by side.

Mr Attwood-Myers was striding quickly and angrily towards the trees, Imran half running to keep up with him. They soon out-distanced the following spectators. As Fredo and his player drew abreast of the trees, Mr Attwood-Myers' ball rose high in the air, missing the branches miraculously, and landed on the green less than half a metre from the hole.

Mr Strydom's second ball hit the green and rolled across into the rough on the far side, costing him a chip shot and a final putt. Mr Attwood-Myers putted cleanly, and he was now only one point behind as they drove off for the eighteenth.

As they stood watching their players tee off, Fredo turned to Imran and said what a good shot Mr Atty had out of the trees.

'Yes, if he had been hitting it with his iron it would have been,' the young Indian frowned. 'I am thinking that Mr Atty would make one damn good fielder if he changed to the cricket game.'

The little Zulu stared at him. 'You mean he...?'

'...picked it up and threw it onto the green. Must I be writing it down for you, Fredo, man? That mission school was wasted.'

Mr Strydom's second shot went to the left of the green, while Mr Attwood-Myers' went even further into the rough. Mr Strydom told Fredo that it wasn't the caddy's fault, for the wind had died just as he hit the ball. Mr Attwood-Myers, on the other hand, blamed Imran for everything, and once again he strode quickly after his ball.

'You go on, Fredo,' Mr Strydom told his caddy. 'I just want to get a stone out of this shoe.'

Leaving his player sitting on the grass untying his shoelace, Fredo hurried away. Something told him to stay close to Mr Atty.

He saw the player pass where Mr Strydom's ball lay, and disappear into the bush. As he drew close he knew his instinct had been correct. Mr Strydom's ball lay pressed deep into the soft soil. As if it had been stepped on by a heavy shoe.

'You there, boy!' he heard Mr Atty call from ahead. 'Come and help us find my damn ball. Quickly, now.'

Fredo left his bag and joined them a few minutes later.

Mr Strydom arrived with the small band of spectators, though his only fan among them was the slim form of Miss Goodhew.

'Oh, what a stroke of luck,' she cried. 'Look, your ball has landed on that little bush.'

The drive from the bush landed only 40 cms from the flag, and a short putt holed it.

Mr Strydom and Fredo waited patiently until Mr Attwood-Myers' ball shot up from the tall bush, curved lazily in the air, and came down in the centre of the green.

To roll slowly forward...and topple down the hole.

There was no sound at first, as everyone gazed in surprise at the empty green. As Mr Attwood-Myers came up the silence was broken by Mr Goodhew's shout of congratulations and the club members thronged around the winner, thumping him on the back and shouting his praises.

Only one person saw the disgusted gesture of the Indian caddy, as he came slowly up to the green. It was like a fielder throwing the ball in from the boundary, but no-one else would have recognised it if they HAD been watching. Except Fredo.

He went over to the despondent Mr Strydom, standing next to Miss Goody who also looked glum, and spoke softly to them both. Their eyes widened, and they smiled at the caddy, and each other.

'One moment,' the firm voice of Mr Strydom carried over the happy crowd. 'I'd like the club president to check the balls, if you please.'

'What the devil for?' Mr Frensham-Smith asked in surprise.

'Surely that's part of the rules, isn't it?' the petite figure at Mr Strydom's elbow snapped loudly. 'That the balls are checked at the end of the game? Why else would you bother to mark them at the beginning of the game?'

'Oh, very well,' the president grumbled as he stooped over the eighteenth hole. He straightened with a look of surprise on his face.

'Well, here's Strydom's ball all right, its marked blue, but the other ball has no red on it. It's not the same ball you started with, old chap, so I'm afraid the game must go to Strydom.'

Fredo grinned as Miss Goody kissed Mr Strydie

A few weeks later the sole topic on the greens and in the clubhouse was the ingratitude of Mr Strydom.

Not only had he eloped with his employer's daughter, he had also persuaded her to use her small savings to help him buy a run-down engineering company. As though that wasn't enough, he'd taken all his blueprints with him, and applied for the patents because Mr Goodhew had never bothered to do so.

'He had a damn good future with old Goodhew,' Mr Frensham-Smith said on the twelfth one day. Fredo was his caddy.

'Ungrateful pup,' the Colonel agreed. 'Sold his soul cheaply for a bit of skirt and a few thousand quid. Silly young sod.'

He handed his club to his caddy, who was Imran, and strolled off with Mr Frensham-Smith, still decrying the shallowness of youth.

'What does that mean?' Fredo asked his friend. '"Selling his soul cheaply?"'

'When a person is doing something dishonest, they are saying that he is selling his soul to the Devil. In Mr Strydie's case I am thinking they confuse dishonest with ingratitude, but they are wrong anyway.'

'And does it make any difference if the reward they get from selling their soul is large or small, Imran?' Fredo asked in his naive way.

His friend shrugged. 'Only that the greater the reward makes the person appear less of a fool for risking it.'

'Well, here are the members of this fine club, who every day risk their souls for bets of a few rand. Or for the sake of winning, and making a good score on their cards. And they call others silly.'

'I know what you are meaning, Fredo,' Imran smiled. 'But what about you and I? When we agree to Mr Frenny's 4, knowing he was 6, or see the Colonel move his ball to a better place, or Mr Atty throw his ball out of the bush; then surely we allow such things for the hope of a R2 tip?'

'You are right,' and Imran was surprised to see him smiling. 'The reward should be worth the loss of the soul.'

They came up to the thirteenth and rested their bags as the two players teed off.

'I was meaning to ask you,' the Indian boy stretched his shoulder muscles. 'How were you so certain that Mr Atty's ball in the hole was not the one he was beginning with, my friend?'

'Mr Strydie asked the same,' Fredo's grin was so huge that his teeth almost filled his entire face. 'It couldn't have been, because it was in my pocket. You remember when Mr Atty told me to look for his ball? Well, I found it.'

The two elderly golf cheats looked around in surprise at the burst of laughter that came from their caddies. Fredo's was the loudest, as he thought of his forthcoming marriage, and the golf lessons he'd been promised by Mr Strydom.

Who had also insisted on giving him R5,000 for helping him win the championship. It was a fortune to the little Zulu, who decided that if you were going to sell your soul anyway, you might as well do it for the right reasons.

And, of course, the right price.

CHAPTER TWO

'Wow, that was *kiff*, eh?' the boy said when the tale was finished, using a word popular among young South Africans to describe something of high quality. 'I had no idea you were such a good storyteller, Joseph.'

'All of my people are *kiff* storytellers,' the old man said solemnly, but there was a twinkle in his eyes. 'Now, my young friend, let us try for sleep again. Today was practice, for tomorrow we begin our journey for real.'

Michael looked at his watch and saw it was still only eight-fifteen, but obediently he lay back down. This time he was asleep within seconds.

He did not know what woke him. It might have been a dream, a night-bird, or the cracking of a twig.

It might also have been the voices, speaking in Zulu.

He saw two shadowy figures rummaging through their gear, and could not prevent himself from shouting as he struggled from his sleeping-bag. The intruders seemed to see him for the first time, and turned, firelight gleaming from the blades in their hands.

Michael finally extricated himself from the bag and stood facing the two thieves.

He was helpless, and all too aware of it. He had nothing to fight with, and no knowledge of how to fight if he had. Fear transfixed and made him shiver at the same time, and he wished desperately for a miracle weapon.

The two thieves grinned at each other, seeing only a child before them, and they began to move in on him.

Suddenly the blanket next to the white boy moved. It was flung off and a terrible battle cry rang through the night stillness. The old man, still dressed in his white man's suit, leapt up with a fighting stick in each hand. They became a blur to the young boy's eyes as they whirled about his head, then suddenly he was moving forward, each arm independent as it took on a separate opponent.

The attackers were young and strong, but they dropped back in awe at the sight of the old man and his sticks. Each found its mark. One whacked to the side of a head, the other cracked down hard on a wrist.

The results of both blows were the same. Knives dropped from hands to the ground, and were followed by those who had held them. Joseph moved in. It had taken no time at all and he stood proudly above his defeated foes. His head tipped back and the old man, throwing off years of humility in the white man's service, gave voice to a victory howl that had its ancient roots not only in the throats of men.

Both thieves stirred, and the old man kicked them to their feet, the one holding his swollen head, the other a shattered wrist. Joseph cursed and reviled them in the Zulu language. 'Warriors do not steal, you are *hyaenas*', his cries rang after them as they crawled away into the night.

The young boy hadn't moved. He'd wished for a miracle weapon and one had arrived. In the shape of his friend Joseph.

'I said I did not like the Xhosa,' the old Ngwane said. 'But twin stick fighting is too good to be left to them alone, and my people borrowed it a long time ago.'

'Won't they be back?'

'No,' the old man said emphatically. 'I know their kind, they are scum. Real men do not steal. They will go back to their *kraal* now, and lick their wounds. Tomorrow we will be gone. Let us go back to bed, Michael.'

'Right,' the young boy agreed. 'And Joseph...I'm glad I'm on your side. You were fantastic.'

The old man felt pride as he laid his head down.

'Once I was a warrior,' he said simply.

They rose early the next morning, ate bread and cold meat which they washed down with water from the stream, and began walking. On this second day, Michael was beginning to feel the weight of his pack but he followed behind Joseph without complaint.

At noon they stopped and lit a small fire, over which Joseph brewed hot tea. Despite the heat of the day, or because of it, it was refreshing. They ate a light meal.

'I suppose they'll be out looking for me by now, but I don't care,' the boy said, as though to himself, then he changed the subject quickly. 'Our teacher told us that the Xhosas used to chop a finger off for some reason.'

'Only the Hintsa tribe,' the old man nodded. 'They cut off the little finger of the left hand when a baby is only three or four months old. Hintsa was a great Xhosa king, and one day he was out hunting leopard. He wounded a big one and it tore off his little finger. Now the Bantu have always been very strict on the custom that a king had to be physically perfect in all ways. Once a king lost a limb,

31

no matter how, he had to step down from the throne and name a successor. This was because no subject must ever be given the chance to think himself better than his king, in any way.'

Joseph puffed away on his pipe, causing small clouds of yellow smoke to hover above his head.

'Hintsa was a good man and a great king, and his people loved him, so they talked it over and came to a strange decision.'

'You mean they...' the boy exclaimed.

'That's right, Michael. They decided to cut off the little finger of every man, woman and child in the tribe, so that no one could claim advantage over the king, and it is still done to this day. Now, it is time to continue our journey, my young friend.'

They moved off, with the boy still musing about the astonishing sacrifice of the Hintsa people.

The day was warm, for spring was turning to summer now, and far off they could see the fields of ripening corn, and the occasional field of cane. Northern Natal was sugar-cane country, but here there were isolated pockets that produced good cane.

Birds were everywhere, from the industrious weaver building his strange hanging nests from branches, to the lazy circling of hawks eyeing their next meal.

It was very still, and the boy could hear strange scampering in the bush to either side. He soon gave up asking the man in front about them, for Joseph would merely chuckle and shake his head.

The day wore on, and gradually the weight of the pack ceased to trouble him. He'd know next time what not to bring, that was for sure. Tins and potatoes. He shook his head at his own stupidity.

Everything around him was a wonder, especially when the old man described things in his own special way, merging the practicality of evolution with the myths of the Bantu people.

Why some birds, like the shrike, sugarbird, *whydah*, and widow, had long tails while others of the same species did not. Why some birds had a melodious voice, and others were raucous and jarred on the ear. What was the purpose in creation for the ugly creatures of the earth? The crocodile, the vulture, the bat? Why must the gentle little *duiker* and *steenbok*, and the *dassie*, be prey to so many predators, including man?

Not all the boy's questions were answered to his satisfaction, but they WERE answered by the man he was with. He could not say the same about his own father, he thought sadly.

Once they saw a family of reedbuck as they crossed open grassland. The buck made his high-pitched sharp whistle and they disappeared. Joseph said there must be water nearby and a few hundred metres further on they came to a still pond, in which they bathed but did not drink.

The day wore on and now they were passing across farmland, keeping to the edges of the sparser crops, or walking through the middle of the corn and cane. Joseph produced a knife and cut off two pieces of cane. They chewed the sweet pulp as they walked.

Michael asked how far it was, and the old man gave his characteristic shrug that could mean many things. He said that depended. As the eagle would fly it was about 230 kilometres to the Cathedral Peak area where his people dwelled. But they did not travel like the eagle and would have to detour around towns, and avoid places of habitation. The going would be slow because of the terrain, and the land would begin to rise as they veered to the north-west.

None the wiser, but guessing it would take them about two weeks at their present rate of progress, Michael was content. The longer the better, as far as he was concerned. What he would do when they got there he didn't really know, but climbing came into it somewhere. He had little equipment of his own, for birthday and Christmas requests were ignored by his father. He would borrow what he needed from the school store for their weekly climbs, so he had only a few slings and nuts with him now. If he did get the chance it would be free climbing. This did not bother him though, for when he was on a climbing face he felt suddenly alive, master of his own destiny.

The gnawing pangs of the classroom were far behind him, and the fear of failure that sat beside him during exams did not apply here. If he peeled off a pitch or lost a hold, he was simply lowered down to begin again. It wasn't failure not to succeed on a climbing face; it was experience for next time.

So the day wore on, both travellers lost in their different thoughts. Joseph, too, was unsure what would happen when they reached their destination. Would his son be alive still? The only son that he had abandoned so long ago. How old would he be now? A man in his middle years for certain, and how many sons and daughters would he have fathered? How many grandchildren did he, Joseph, have that he had never laid eyes on?

The same questions assailed him now that had done so for more years that he cared to recall. He had always sent money to the village, in care for his son, and without a return address, so he never knew if it reached its destination.

Over the years the salve to his conscience had never been a burden, for he had never married again and begun another family. There had been women, of course, but only for his immediate gratification.

Never anything more, for Mutati had been his first and last love. And until the day he died it would be so.

'You told me the Amangwane are descended from the Zulu,' the boy asked. 'But where does the word Zulu come from?'

'About three hundred years ago, the Nguni migration moved into what is now *kwaZulu*,' the old man answered. 'One small group was led by Malandela, and they lived in the valley of the Mhlanthuze River. When he died his elder son took over, but a younger son left to find his own place in the sun. His name was Zulu, meaning 'Heaven'.

'He settled in the valley of the Mkhumbane, and they grazed cattle, goats and sheep, and grew sorghum, gourds, sweet potatoes and other crops. Life was good for the *abakwaZulu* - the people of Zulu - during this quiet and peaceful time, and Zulu was buried there.

'The generations had increased by the time Senzangakhona became chief, and the valley was their whole world. Angry because his son failed to stop a wild dog attacking one of his sheep, the chief banished him from his sight. The boy was aged only six. He grew up with a burning ambition for greatness, and became commander of one of Dingiswayo's regiments. When his father died he became chief of the Zulus, and from a handful of people in a shallow valley he formed one of the greatest armies ever seen. His name was Chaka.'

A large fire burned that night, and to his relief they used more of Michael's heavy tinned food. Potatoes were sliced and fried, and tinned sausages added. Peaches and condensed milk followed, and the boy smiled at the appreciative way the old man scraped his plate, for one of the few vices of old age is a sweet tooth.

The meal was eaten from plates Michael had brought, part of their combined kitchen that had caused much laughter on their item check. Without getting together, they had two plates and two mugs, and while Michael boasted a full cutlery set, Joseph ate everything with a spoon and his sheath knife. He had planned to eat everything straight from the pot, but accepted the luxury of a plate as more to his liking.

After the meal, the pot was cleaned and fresh water was put on to boil for tea. The old man's pipe came out, and the boy knew it was time for another tale. All that was required was prompting.

'Do you know anything of lost cities, Joseph?' he asked casually. 'They say the big glitzy one in Bophuthatswana is based on a real one somewhere in Africa.'

The old man chuckled. 'There are always stories of lost things, *jong*. Lost gold mines, lost treasure, lost diamonds... lost cities. But some are true. Take the Ma-Iti, and their fabulous city in the north.'

The boy waited impatiently while the pipe was scraped clean, refilled, and puffed to a good draw.

CHAPTER THREE

THE LOST CITY OF THE MA-ITI

More than two thousand years ago, the old man related in his own way, a group of Bantu boys were playing on the banks of the Zambesi, when they saw a strange sight.

Hiding in the bushes they saw a huge canoe sail past. Along its side ran two rows of long paddles. A great sheet of skin was stretched on a long stick that hung on many ropes across a tall pole in the centre of the big canoe. Three great knives were attached to the front end, and there was a carving shaped like a man with hair that resembled a lion's mane.

The men who sailed the great canoe looked like devils to the watching boys, for they wore helmets and leggings of bronze, with breastplates of bronze scales.

Each man was heavily armed, with shields either of leather studded with iron and bronze, or of iron with bronze bosses. They carried heavy iron-headed spears and wore swords at their sides.

Shipping their long paddles they brought the canoe to a halt, threw off their clothes and jumped naked into the river to swim and bathe. The little boys were terrified, for the strangers were pink all over. Like the figure on the prow of the ship they had hair like the manes of lions, falling to their shoulders. Some had hair as black and shiny as a panther, some red as fire. One or two had hair the colour of autumn corn.

As the boys ran swiftly to their village with news of the strangers, little were they aware that their lives were to change for ever, and the Bantu would not know peace again for many lifetimes. If ever.

It was the start of a lost empire - the empire of the people called the Ma-Iti. The place they came from sounded like 'Iti' to the Bantu, for Ma-Iti means 'people from Iti', but in fact it was Gatti. Today we know them as the Phoenicians.

Stories about them are still told around the cooking fires in South and Central Africa. Badly rusted and crumbling swords of ancient Greek manufacture, old gold coins and parts of bronze shields and helmets, bronze spears and Egyptian battle axes; all are still kept secretly by witchdoctors, and they confirm the truth of the stories about a white race that invaded Southern Africa.

Five hundred years before Christ.

The pink-skinned strangers traded steel and bronze weapons - spears, knives, axes - for corn and milk, but only through one man. Lumbedu the witchdoctor. Lumbedu was ambitious, and when he had accumulated a hoard of these metal weapons he waged war on his neighbours, easily routing whole armies armed only with bone-tipped spears and stone axes. His band of cut-throats overthrew the High Chief of the land in a day and Lumbedu became ruler in his stead.

Intoxicated with power, the new High Chief asked the Ma-Iti for more weapons, which they gave him, and his fierce armies raged across the land, conquering every tribe they found. Soon Lumbedu had become the undisputed monarch of the biggest empire the Bantu had ever seen, for it stretched from the Inyangani Mountains to the shores of the Western Ocean.

But it was an empire that belonged to Lumbedu the witchdoctor for just one year and eight moons.

The cunning Ma-Iti had planned well. They waited until every other tribe in the land had been conquered, and the ruffianly army was drunk and disorganised, and then they struck swiftly. Lumbedu was killed, his men routed, and his *kraal* burned to the ground. By killing one fat traitor of his people, the Ma-Iti had in turn become rulers of hundreds of thousands of Bantu, and a huge empire.

The people became the slaves of the white men, long lines of men, women and children chained together like beads on a necklace, hauling sleds of stones to build great forts all across the land.

Thousands more were forced to live beneath the earth, digging for iron ore, copper, and the yellow metal of the sun. The Sacred Iron Mountain of Taba-Zimbi was turned into a mass of tunnels, where tens of thousands lived, worked and died.

Long caravans of oxen and trained zebras wound their way eastward over mountains and across plains, heavily laden with gold, iron ore and ivory, to be loaded on the ships of the Ma-Iti and taken away to their land across the seas. Many Bantu slaves went also, and were never seen again.

Elephant and hippo, sacred to nearly all the tribes, were slaughtered by the Ma-Iti. The elephant for its ivory and the hippo for its bones and blubber. The cruelty, bloodshed and carnage, to man and beast alike, went on and on.

The Ma-Iti made great plantations near the Inyangani Mountains, and thousands of slaves planted, hoed and reaped corn and other crops which the Ma-Iti had brought from their native land.

Even today, traces of these fantastic plantations - which legends say were fertilised during winter with the hacked bodies of dead slaves - still survive. They are known as the terraced plantations of Inyanga, yet no black people have ever farmed in the terraced style.

More of the Ma-Iti came to settle in the land of the Bantu, together with members of that hated race called the Arabi, who would wreak much havoc in the land in the years to follow.

Fifty years after the death of Lumbedu, the Ma-Iti began to build many cities, the biggest and most important of which was on the shores of Lake Makarikari, which today is a vast shallow pan.

More than a thousand people lived in that city, according to legend, and it was considered impregnable to attack. Stone towers guarded it at regular intervals, and a deep water-filled ditch surrounded it completely. The only entry into the city was over a short wooden bridge across the ditch into a gateway.

As a result of the trade with lands beyond the waters, the Ma-Iti gathered fantastic wealth around them, and they lived in great luxury. Besides the weapons and armour there are unbelievably old ornaments of gold and silver and bronze - ornaments that are neither Bantu or Arabi; worn, pitted, some even distorted by age - and they are jealously guarded today by tribal historians and witchdoctors as the secret charms of the tribe. They are still used in secret rituals and keep the Ma-Iti tales fresh in the story-tellers' minds.

Like many empires of the past, the Ma-Iti turned decadent, becoming isolated from the outside world. Their attention turned to making their lives as full of luxury and pleasure as possible. Life became one long orgy. They invented new and fantastic ways of entertainment, and had idols before which they performed rites both revolting and awesome.

The legends say that some of the queens and empresses began mating with beasts, and some even tried to mate their daughters to lions to produce a new race of men who would combine the courage, endurance and ferocity of lions with the intelligence of human beings. The legends also speak of an emperor of the Ma-Iti who had a young man for his queen, and this queen used to kill women, both of his own race and the Bantu, with great cruelty and merely for his entertainment.

The saviour of the Bantu was Lumukanda, one of the greatest heroes of Bantu folklore. He was born a slave, of slave parents, in one of the filthy underground stalls in the great city on the shores of Lake Makarikari, where men were forced to live like beasts. He was only sixteen summers, but a young giant, immensely strong and trained in swordplay for the entertainment of his masters.

The Ma-Iti empire was weakened at that time by a war between two rival emperors, and Lumukanda took advantage of the turmoil in the city to escape with many other slaves. He then led a vast army of Bantu and Bushmen against the oppressors of his people. City after city fell to him, but the great city on the shores of Lake Makarikari, with its wide moat and high walls, and thousands of fierce defenders, remained seemingly impregnable.

They crossed the moat on great rafts, carrying ladders with which to scale the high walls, but the mighty throwing machines of the defenders sank raft after raft with a hail of stones. If it was possible to take the city at all, then it could only be at a tremendous loss of life.

Then Lumukanda was sent a plan by the Gods. He withdrew his forces, and for the rest of the day thousands of men worked in the nearby forest, digging a tunnel towards the city under cover of the thick bush, while others, Bantu blacksmiths, worked tirelessly forging more and more tools for the digging. All had worked for many years, some all their lives, in the Ma-Iti mines, and by sunset were three-quarters of the way to the city that could not be taken.

By dawn the tunnel was complete, and while some of the army attacked the outside walls of the city to distract the defenders, Lumukanda led the rest through the tunnel. They emerged in the centre of the city, unnoticed, and men who had known a lifetime of suffering and humiliation showed no mercy. The carnage was sickening, as Ma-Iti men, women and children ran screaming through the streets, the Bantu warriors chasing them, blood-crazy now, with the long-haired heads of their victims impaled on their spears.

The massacre did not stop until no Ma-Iti was left alive.

True to the vow he had once made, Lumukanda ordered the city to be demolished. For three whole days, tens of thousands of Bantu, Bushmen and half-castes laboured, razing temples, towers and houses to the ground, and scattering the stones over the countryside.

Everything which was not breakable, like armour, metal vessels, bronze statues - even gold and silver ornaments - were taken into the forest and melted down. Yet against Lumukanda's orders many articles disappeared as trophies of the victorious army of former slaves.

By the fourth day, all that could be seen of the city was the big oblong clearing which had been the Great Square, some traces of streets and some foundations of houses. These too would disappear under the ravages of wind and weather - and time. Lumukanda's vow was made good.

A new and mighty nation was founded from the ashes of the invaders; the Lu-Anda, which means 'they that increase'. Together with the Ba-Kongo people, this nation ruled vast tracts of land from the shores of the Western Ocean to Ka-Tanga, which today is called Shaba in the country of Zaire.

'I see, then they began to move south,' Michael said when he was sure the old man had finished. 'And that's where the Zulu and Xhosa come from, and the Venda, and the Sothu, and Swazi, and the...'

Joseph held up his hand and smiled. 'Please, we save that for another time. It is long, and we need our sleep now. There are many miles for our shoes to eat tomorrow.'

'You're right,' Michael smiled, and crawled into his sleeping bag. 'Goodnight, Joseph. And thank you.'

'Goodnight, *jong*,' the old man said with affection, *jong* being an Afrikaans word for young man. He did not need to ask what the thanks were for.

He knew it was not for the reciting of a story.

CHAPTER FOUR

They arose at dawn, a habit that Michael had fallen into easily, and he could not believe how much more could be fitted into the day with those extra hours.

Joseph blew the embers of their fire alight while the boy gathered wood. When he returned, he was handed a stick with a slice of bread on the end and he grinned and sat toasting it and getting warm at the same time. After he'd done several pieces, Joseph asked solemnly, 'Hard or soft? One or two?'

The boy gave him a puzzled look, and the old man gave his deep chuckle of amusement. He took the pot off the fire and showed it to Michael. Inside were half a dozen boiled eggs.

The boy grinned happily, and was about to reach in when his face clouded. 'But where...?'

'Do not ask, Michael,' he smiled. 'But I will tell you this, I never take more than two from any nest. Now eat, unless you...'

The boy reached in quickly and took two out.

They were delicious and he completely forgot where they came from as he ate. If there were any post-digestion qualms they did not show.

Joseph found a track that cut across the open *veldt* they now found themselves on, and it was wide enough for them to walk side by side.

'That story you told me last night, Joseph,' Michael said after a little while. 'What about all the treasures from the other Ma-Iti cities? And the stuff that came from the lost one itself?'

'There are many hoards of treasure buried deep in this continent of ours, Michael,' came the reply. 'The legends say there are ten *Pato ya Ma-Iti* - treasure hoards of the Ma-Iti - scattered across the lands of the Bantu. They are known only to a few Chosen Ones and some High Witchdoctors.'

'Wow,' the boy breathed. 'If only we could find one. I bet it would be worth a fortune. But wouldn't that be sacrilege to you, Joseph?'

'No, Michael,' the grizzled head shook. 'Many years ago I lived in a mission, where I became a Christian. They taught me many things, like reading and writing, and how to add figures and take them away from each other. They also taught me about the Christian God, and how different he is from the legends of my people.'

'I wish I'd gone to that mission,' the boy said miserably. 'I'm sure you can speak better English than me if you want to. Fanagalo is all right, but you're the only one I can speak it to.'

'It is not true Fanagalo, *jong*,' the old man smiled. 'It is something we have put together ourselves, from Afrikaans and English and Zulu. And no, I cannot speak better English than you, just as you cannot speak better Zulu than me, for it is the language I was born with, but even so, there are differences in Ngwane.'

'There are differences in everything,' the boy sighed. 'And I always pick up the wrong difference when I write exams.'

'Do not mind, Michael,' the old man laughed. 'You are in my schoolroom now, and so far you are doing very well. Top of the class I think.'

'Right,' the boy said sarcastically. 'As the only student I suppose I have to be,' but he was pleased, and the old man knew that.

'How did your people first come to settle in the Drakensberg, Joseph?' Michael asked that night.

They had eaten well once more, for the old man had made *putu* from the mealie meal, and added meat and a tin of beans, with curry paste to flavour. While the water was brewing for the inevitable tea Joseph produced his battered corncob pipe, which Michael now knew to be the prelude to a lengthy tale. He settled down on his sleeping bag and threw a few thick branches on the fire.

THE FIRST BANTU IN THE DRAKENSBERG

The first Bantu people to settle in the Natal Drakensberg were the Amazizi, Joseph puffed away as he began his story, in the area between the Upper Tugela and the Bushman's River. The Bushmen must have been alarmed when they saw these black men arrive, and they pushed higher into the Little Berg, with the sandstone cliffs forming a natural boundary.

The new arrivals were pastoralists, however. In the foothills, along the river valleys, the Amazizi built their beehive grass huts with much care. They were soon tilling the land and their herdsmen grazed their cattle on the lush grasslands.

They did not interfere with the Bushmen, who were hunters, and they managed to live in harmony. The Amazizi took bushwomen as their wives and barter was common between the two groups.

Elsewhere the war clouds were gathering over the Bantu peoples. Dingiswayo's Mtetwa *iMpe's* attacked the Amangwane, for he heard that their leader, Matiwane, was growing in power. Warned of the attack, the Amangwane gave their cattle to Mtimkulu of the Amahlubi to look after, and offered little resistance before surrendering to Dingiswayo.

The Mtetwa departed, leaving the defeated army almost intact, and Matiwane called on Mtimkulu to return his cattle, but the chief of the Amahlubi refused. Matiwane was hesitant about attacking them because of the rugged terrain in which they lived, and while he held back Zwide and his Ndwandwe warriors took advantage and launched a furious attack on the Amangwane.

They were again defeated but this time they were left without homes, food or cattle. Now Matiwane had no option and attacked Mtimkulu's royal *kraal,* killing everyone including the chief. The rest of the Amahlubi fled in terror, many climbing the steep passes of the Drakensberg and making their way into Lesotho.

They had lost everything and were forced to attack and rob the Sutu clans to feed themselves.

Matiwane and his people marched north and the black war clouds turned red as they savagely attacked all in their path. Matiwane himself plucked out the gall bladders of the fallen chiefs and drank the contents, hoping to strengthen his courage. He also attacked the peaceful Amazizi, who fled south along the foothills to Pondoland, and north in the path of Titizizi. Others hid in the deep valleys of the Berg with the Bushmen.

Matiwane and his Amangwane, now tired of war, settled beneath the mighty *kwaMdedelele* - Cathkin Peak - and peace returned to the valleys of the Berg. The hoe replaced the spear and they built their huts with the tall Tambookie grass, and tilled the soil and grazed their cattle.

They had become farmers once more.

Their pastoral existence was short-lived. Dingiswayo and Zwide were now dead, but a greater menace was approaching the Drakensberg. One day the Amangwane watched in fear as a black mass moved towards them on the eastern horizon.

Chaka, son of Senzangakhona, had become chief of the Zulu clan with the help of his mentor, Dingiswayo. Two years later, on the death of Dingiswayo, he had also taken over chieftainship of the Mtetwa. Chaka had merged both tribes into a powerful nation, and added to them from the best of the tribes he defeated.

Now his *iMpe's* were approaching kwaMdedelele.

The Amangwane, soft now with their peaceful life, were no match for the disciplined and fearless warriors who made up the invincible Zulu army. Once again Matiwane and his people fled, and only the mighty range of *uKhahlamba* could protect them. The Barrier of Spears guarded the summits jealously as the Amangwane fled across the Tugela valley below Mont-aux-Sources, and over the Basuto Gate into LeSuthu.

Thus began the Wars of the Mfecane, when more than a hundred thousand died in battle. Food became scarce and cannibalism was rife. Eventually Matiwane, now a broken man, followed the long trail to Zululand, and arrived at the Royal Kraal to find that Chaka was dead and Dingana (wrongly called Dingaan by the Whites), was now on the throne.

Fearing the worst from this short fat man, who could order the most terrible punishments yet would himself vomit at the sight of blood, Matiwane told his son, Zikhali, to remain behind and gave him the brass arm-ring of chieftain. He and his few followers proceeded on to visit Dingana.

His fears were well founded, and all were slain on a hill known today as Matiwane's Hill. Matiwane's eyes were gouged out and wooden pegs driven up his nostrils.

With a perversity typical of him, Dingana took a liking to the son of the man he'd just slain, and spared his life providing he joined his Zulu army. So Zikhali served in the *umKhulutshane* regiment.

When Dingana was finally overthrown, Zikhali fled to Swaziland where he met King Sobuza's daughter, Nomlalazi. But the King was not happy about their romance, and Zikhali returned to Mdedelele, the place he remembered where the Amangwane had lived for four peaceful years in the foothills of the Drakensberg.

Nomlalazi followed, and as the fragmented tribesmen heard the news of their chief's return, gradually the broken tribe came back to the place of their dreams.

But far away the wagon-wheels were creaking, as the *Voortrekkers* began their migration to the north, and the country below the Barrier of Spears would be changed for ever.

CHAPTER FIVE

As usual when Joseph finished a tale there was a companionable silence while each recounted it in his mind. For Joseph there was satisfaction that he still remembered the stories he'd heard in his youth. For the young white boy there was the magic of times gone by, history that he'd learned in school now suddenly come alive when seen through other eyes.

The eyes of a black man.

'Have you had many wives, Joseph?' the boy asked one morning as they sat finishing their tea.

'Many women,' the old man replied, and began to light his pipe. 'But only one wife. She was the most beautiful and best wife a man could want.'

There was a pause as he sucked deeply to open up the hole in the stem. It was time to replace the old pipe, he knew, but he was reluctant to part with the companion of so many years. If only Mutati could have been his companion for half so many years...

LOBOLA

To qualify for marriage a man must first have gone through the tribal initiation, and have raised the *lobola*, or bride-price.

Part of that initiation is circumcision. It is very painful, as the blade goes back and forth though the young boy's foreskin to remove it, the old man said, concealing the mirth deep inside as he saw the horrified expression on his young friend's face.

The warriors watch closely to observe the boy's reaction, and he recalled how relieved he'd been when it was over, and there was no criticism of him. He had felt the pain and had come close to crying, but the thought that he must be brave and endure had given him courage.

'This is a man', they had all said, and his pride was almost too much to bear.

It took him nearly two years to raise enough *lobola* to pay Mutati's father for her hand in marriage, but there came the day when he led the two cows and four goats into her father's *kraal*, and a date was agreed for the marriage.

On the day of the wedding there was much excitement in the valleys as the guests gathered at the groom's home, where a flag flew from the top of a bamboo pole to announce the occasion. Joseph was dressed in trappings similar to a Zulu warrior - furs, skins, a head-dress and anklets - and he proudly displayed his cowhide shield and favourite fighting sticks.

The wedding guests were in full array, especially the newly married girls who must stand in *hlonipha* attitude, leaning on a beaded stick, one foot forward, and with a remote detached expression on their faces. The moment for which the guests had been waiting arrived, and the bride and her maidens came to the groom's *kraal*, and bathed in a nearby stream. They advanced in a dancing, chanting group to the groom and his party of menfolk, seated in an open space in front of his *kraal*.

Dressed only in a skirt, with beads around her neck and an elaborate hair-do, Mutati solemnly and respectfully approached her future husband's home. Around her waist was a band made of plaited grass, a token of eternity. In her hand she carried the knife; traditionally a short stabbing spear, and token of virginity.

Mutati first threatens him with it, then challenges him, and finally hands it symbolically to her groom amidst loud shouts and applause. Much drinking, eating and dancing follows, and the guests discuss the couple. The beer gourds pass freely as the guests drink copiously, and far into the night laughter and singing is heard in the valleys of uKhahlamba.

By now Mutati had been garbed as a married woman, with the black leather skirt, the ochre topknot and grass belt; all symbolic of her new status. Her bride's box had come on the heads of her maidens, and she had opened this with the key on a string of white beads kept around her neck. From it, beads would be taken to decorate her.

So had begun the most wonderful time of Joseph's life. He tended his father's cattle, hunted with his friends in the hills; and came back each evening to his beehive hut, and Mutati his bride. After a year his son was born, and his star had reached its zenith. He asked for nothing from the Gods.

To test his spirit, that was what they left him. Nothing.

Mutati died of a fever when his son was only three years old. Sick at heart, Joseph, then still known by his tribal name of Kqwedi, had left his son in the charge of his father's wives and set out on his travels.

The travels that were to last for many years of his life, until he found his place with the old *baas* in the city of the Whites by the sea.

'That's a very sad story,' Michael said softly. 'It's sadder knowing it's true, and happened to someone I know. Why have you never seen your son since? '

The old man rose stiffly, and the weight of his years seemed to lay heavier with the question, which he did not really answer. 'I have never seen my village since that day.'

He began to walk off, and the young boy quickly poured the rest of the tea over the embers of the fire, kicked dirt on to make sure it was out, and hurried after him.

Joseph seemed changed during the next few days. The innocent question from the boy had placed his own past actions firmly before him. Rather, lack of actions. The same question in its various forms he had asked himself often, increasingly in recent years.

They were now in high, rolling hill country, covered with plantations and rich, grassy farmland. At noon they stopped and Joseph brewed up without a word. Faithful to the old man's mood, Michael said nothing and sipped his tea in silence.

The afternoon was peaceful, and the lack of conversation between the two travellers was welcome to both. Joseph was wrapped in his own morose thoughts, while the boy could not get enough of the sights around him.

The old man stopped abruptly and Michael, watching a pair of jackal buzzards circling lazily above their heads, nearly ran into him. Joseph held his head to one side, in an intent listening pose, then the young lad heard it too.

Abrupt *perrips*, or musical chucks could be heard faintly, and holding a finger to his lips Joseph moved off silently to the left. Picking their way carefully through the *fynbos* they came upon a small clearing, where a startling sight greeted them.

A dark brown snake was reared up with hood expanded, cobra fashion. Its length was nearly 100 centimetres, and its hood moved slowly around as it kept its two opponents in view. These were each about a third its size, also dark brown though grizzled with white or buff, and with faces like short-eared mice.

'Rinkals,' the old man said softly. 'Very dangerous, Michael. It is a front-fanged snake, and as well as giving a poisonous bite, it can spit venom. If it goes in your eyes it can blind you. It is far from its home here, for uKhahlamba is where it lives.'

'Are they mongooses attacking it?' the boy whispered.

Joseph nodded. 'They are dwergmuishond - dwarf mongoose. They will have their home beneath ground here, and I think the rinkals might have gone down after their young. No matter, the mongoose kills the snake whenever he sees it.'

As though on cue, the two little beasts moved on the snake from either side. Its head reared back even further, and three pale bands could be seen on its throat. The little fellow on the right darted in at its tail, but the hood dipped down with a speed that the boy's eyes found hard to follow.

The mongoose had been expecting it, and ran on without paying any attention to the tail. As the snake's head went down, the other little chap went straight in for the back of its neck. The sharp little teeth fastened tightly and kept the jaws immobile, allowing the mongoose's partner to come back to help. It moved in below its mate and attacked the snake's spine with its claws. Those on the forefeet were long, curved and adapted to scratching and digging, and they made short work of tearing back the skin to reveal the white vertebrae.

Still the other little mongoose kept a firm grip on its neck, while the snake struggled ineffectively to free itself. Unable to move its great hooded head, it threw the length of its body around instead.

But by now the first little creature had almost bitten through the spine. The result of the extravagant movement on the part of the snake was that its back snapped like a dry twig. The other, worrying the neck like a terrier, succeeded in biting right through it.

By mutual decision, the two withdrew to watch the snake in its death throes. Other small brown shapes had appeared, and stood still as though in homage to their brave fellows.

'Will they eat it now?' Michael asked, then realised he'd used his normal voice as the sharp *chuchwee* of their alarm call rang out. The pack froze, then quietly scuttled off to cover.

'Yes, if they are allowed to,' the old man chuckled. 'Come, they deserve to be left alone.'

They returned to their path, and continued to the west.

The rest of the day passed without further incident and they stopped in a small stand of trees ten minutes before dusk fell. By the time the lengthening shadows had merged with the anonymity of night, wood had been collected and the bivouac erected. A good cooking fire was sending leaping flames into the sky and the pot and pan were ready to go on when it had settled.

After they'd eaten, and the supper things had been cleaned up, the pipe came out and the evening ritual commenced. The peace was suddenly shattered by a maniacal cackle, a series of drawn-out who-o-oops, rising in pitch and trailing out in low moans.

'Joseph, what...?' but the boy's words were cut short by more strange sounds from the far side of the woods. Grunts and groans were interspersed with giggles, yells and whines.

Michael was white-faced as he turned frightened eyes on the old man. Joseph was still calmly drawing smoke through the congested bowl of the ancient cob. He appeared not to have heard anything unusual.

'Hyaena,' he said finally. 'Two or more, and they have maybe found an injured buck, or killed some small creature. Like the rinkals they are not usually so far south. The drought perhaps has sent them here.'

'Will they attack us? During the night?' the boy asked.

'No, their bellies will be full soon, but a hyena will only make his own kill if he is desperate. Sometimes an old one will take a small child from a kraal but it is not usual. There are many legends of the hyena being evil, and a creature of the tokoloshe, because he feeds at night and his strange cries put fear in men.'

'Like it did to me, just now,' the boy's tone was self-deprecatory. 'I'm glad I'm not on my own. I've heard of the tokoloshe too. It's different to different tribes. The Zulu thinks it's a creature that lives under your bed, and comes out at night to attack you, so they build their beds up on bricks sometimes. The people who live in the mountains of Lesotho are afraid of the dark because they see him as a little man covered in hair.'

Joseph laughed and used his pipe to stab the air to emphasis his words. 'That is right. The thokolosi of the Suthu is very mischievous and torments women. He can also do a lot of harm and lives in pools at the bottom of waterfalls, and that is why the people who live there seldom go near those pools.'

'Do YOU believe in them, Joseph?' the boy asked.

'I believe in them because they are real, and I have seen one when I was a young man,' his face was solemn. 'But it was not the tokoloshe of the legends. They were human men who were given drugs by the witchdoctors, so they would obey their orders. The people of Africa who were carried to the West Indies as slaves, long ago, also do this. There is a word for it, a zom...?'

'Zombie,' Michael remembered. 'The living dead. They're supposed to be dead people that are brought back to life to obey Baron Samedi, the Lord of the Dead.'

Again the old man chuckled. 'Some of your schooling is not wasted, I think. Though perhaps your father would want you to learn other things.'

'I'm interested in it,' Michael admitted. 'I know maths and stuff are useful, but they're boring. Do you know any ghost stories, Joseph?'

'I know many stories,' the old man said carefully. 'The listener himself must decide if they are spirit stories or not. The hyena reminds me of another beast of the night, and also a legend among my people.'

He began scraping the bowl of his pipe and repacking it with the harsh tobacco he favoured. The boy waited patiently, and was slowly aware that the sounds in the woods behind them had ceased.

CHAPTER SIX

THE TIME OF THE ANIMALS

It was many years ago, following the time of the animals, Joseph began. Now was the time of the White, not the Black; but unlike the animals, the black man's time would come again.

The annihilation of the animals came about at an alarming rate, entire herds being decimated during a single shoot. Only a person who had seen those herds could imagine the numbers, or could begin to realise the horror - and the terrible waste.

It was not to provide food for the pot like the genuine hunter or *voortrekker*, but for the pelts and skins, the horns of solidified hair, and the tusks of ivory. Rich hunters from lands across the seas would also come, to kill for reasons other than money. They cut off heads and dug out horns and tusks to hang on their walls, and skinned beautiful pelts to use as rugs. Trophies of the hunt they called them, and these pieces of dead animals made them proud.

There were the butchers who hunted mercilessly and relentlessly, shooting anything that moved. Greed was the usual motivator in such men - but not always. Some desired only to kill.

As recently as the mid-19th century there were vast herds of game to be found in the middle of Natal and along the foothills of the Drakensberg. The *springbok* treks over the vast plains of the Free State were well documented, and it was estimated that, '10,000 springbok could stand on an acre, and 10,000 acres were covered by a moving mass of *trekbokke* as far as the eye could see on all sides.'

There must have been 100 million animals on the Natal *veldt* alone. *Quagga, wildebeest,* zebra, lion, elephant, buffalo, leopard, hippopotami, and numerous herds of antelope. The herds would come down from the Orange Free State, trekking into the warmer *thornveldt* during April and May - and would take all day to pass one point.

With the coming of the Whites, much changed. The game was killed off in the areas around the towns, then in the outlying parts. Finally the hunters moved to the more distant areas, such as the remote fastnesses of the Drakensberg.

The black man also played his part in the slaughter of the animals that had been his bounty, yet made little from it except the few bright beads and trinkets that were cast in his direction. The Black worked for the White in many ways; tracking for him, hauling his equipment on safari, cleaning the results of his outrages, and carrying the rich booty back to his outposts.

Great Africa mourned the departed spirits of its animals, destined for extinction because of the white man's greed and avarice - and the hunter's never-ending desire for glory. Elephant, rhino, buffalo; and the great cats of the high and low *veldt.* All through Southern Africa they would be gone over the next ten decades, the remaining few trapped behind fences of reserves and game farms.

But that was the future, and when had the past ever cared for the future?

A few years before the beginning of the end, a famous hunter came into the land of the Zulu. He had hunted those parts before and he knew what was expected of him, for he took many gifts to please the great Zulu king.

The huge fat king sat on a throne piled high with leopard skins, and he wore a full robe of lion pelt. The hollow head of the proud beast covered his baldness.

The king was pleased with the gifts of the white hunter.

Permission to hunt was granted with an imperious wave of the royal hand, emerald and ruby fire blazing from the jewelled rings handed down through the royal line.

Unlike many who visited the king's royal *kraal*, the grey-bearded hunter did not covert the gold and jewels of the Zulu king. Gold from the ancient mines of Great Zimbabwe, the white stones from the edge of the sea to the west, and the coloured stones from the hated Arabi in exchange for their own people as slaves.

No, the hunter had already made many fortunes by exchanging baubles of little value for the black man's gold and precious stones, and even bigger fortunes from the beasts that roamed his land.

Now wealth meant little to him any more.

Not since his woman had left, following the death of their only child. The child that he'd taken on the hunt, insisting it would make a man of him, against his wife's pleas that he was too gentle a creature to kill.

On that, his first hunt, the mother's words had been proven right, in tragic fashion.

The boy's finger had frozen on the trigger, and the father's shot had been inches away from the perfect kill he'd made so many times before. The water-buffalo, the deadliest of the big five of Africa, had stamped the boy into the rich loam of the *veldt*.

After that, instead of terminating the kind of life that had caused the tragedy, he had pursued it even more. His tally was prodigious. Over 400 lion, nearly 200 leopard, 100 cheetah, nearly 700 elephant, 500 rhino, and so many buffalo that he'd lost count. From his walls hung the greatest heads, and on his floors lay the finest skins. The accolades of fellow hunters rang in his ears to feed his ego and arrogance.

Despite his years of killing the best of the continent's creatures, he found no affinity with them - and no compassion. It was as though each new kill brought a greater hatred for the beasts he'd once respected - even as he'd killed them. For like an old beast himself, the white man had gone rogue.

This was to be his ultimate quest - for his most magnificent trophy.

It would also be his last hunt.

The morning they were to set out the king contemptuously ordered the white hunter's bearers back to their *kraals* near the coast, and replaced them with many of his finest warriors.

Among those pressed into the service of the grey-beard was a young man named Fikizolo, which meant, 'he came yesterday'. At the time his mother was due his father was away fighting with the king's army. He was commander of an *iMpe*, and fought fiercely and bravely to be back for the birth. But when he arrived home he was told, '*fikizolo*', and such was the name he gave his son.

Fikizolo was a soldier in the Leopard *iMpe*, his father's old regiment. He was very proud of this, for the Leopards were the best warriors in the army. He had seen nineteen summers, and would one day be married to the girl promised to him when both were babies.

She was called Manatise, after a great chieftainess of the *baTlonkwa* tribe. She was as fierce as her namesake, and Fikizolo filled with a pride that made his heart want to burst when he saw her. The same heart that ached when he thought of the time he would have to wait before he could save the *lobola* to claim her.

So it was with great interest that he listened to the words of the white man, when they made camp that first night on the *veldt*. The grey-beard spoke the Zulu language well, but only a few sentences were needed to convey his message.

He would give twenty head of cattle to the man who led him to what he sought. Fikizolo's eyes became rounder and wider at such wealth. Ten head was his bride-price, and already he had four. He used his fingers and toes to calculate. With fourteen cows he would be one of the wealthiest men in the *kraal*, second only to the fathers of the prettiest daughters who commanded the best dowries.

Then, as though from another fire on a distant *veldt*, he heard what the reward was for. What creature it was that the hunter sought.

The white leopard.

They would follow the Tugela, the white man was saying.

Towards the great mountain range that the Dutchmen had named *Draaksberge*, and was known to the Zulu as *uKhahlamba* - the Barrier of Uplifted Spears. The mountains were the haunt of the spotted cat and that was where the whiteskin hoped to find his prey.

The words continued but the young warrior was elsewhere.

His mind had travelled to the past, to his year of manhood. When he had been taken to the foothills and left on his own to hunt his manhood trophy. He had climbed that day and all of the next, and found no trace of spoor.

Before darkness fell he found a small green valley sheltering among the rocky peaks. He lodged for the night in a lone acacia, grown sturdily independent in blissful ignorance of its unusual height above the tree line. Fikizolo tied himself firmly into a fork and fell into an exhausted, uneasy, and uncomfortable sleep.

As the sun began to appear above *uKhahlamba*, throwing fingers of light and casting long shadows down the slopes, the young Zulu came awake. He began to untie himself, then stiffened.

The distinctive rasping cough came from above and behind him. From the same tree he perched upon. It was familiar despite that he'd never seen a live leopard before. But many times around the fire he'd heard the hunters imitate its call.

Slowly Fikizolo turned his head. The sight that met his eyes made him close them again, quickly, and his lips moved in silent entreaty to his favourite gods.

It was the biggest leopard he'd ever heard of, and it was stretched out on a branch only the length of a paw above his head. One downward swipe could have taken his face off, though it did not appear threatening. Indifferent rather than vicious. Still, the apprentice warrior was petrified with fright.

For it was not like the skins on the king's throne, which were pale to golden yellow, with black spots and rosettes. It was white, and its eyeballs were a dark pink, almost red. The pupils were pure black. This creature was of the night-spirit himself. Surely it was the *tokoloshe* in the guise of a leopard.

The youth willed himself to turn and face the creature, and his cowering stopped as he looked into the incredible depths of pink and black. He did not stare defiantly, for although his fear waned after a moment, he knew that would have been foolish. Instead he gazed as an equal.

They stayed that way until the sun had climbed well over the mountains and the whole valley was covered by its glow. Then the albino leopard came upright on its narrow perch, and powerful muscles and sinews vied for prominence as the magnificent animal stretched luxuriously, like any house cat.

When it had finished, the black-within-pink eyes turned on the figure below, and a soft purr came from its throat as Fikizolo spoke softly to it.

'Truly you are a wondrous creation, my white leopard. Forgive me for thinking you a creature of the night-spirit, for how could that be when you are as white as the clouds above *uKhahlamba*, and they belong to the god of the day.'

The leopard's cough rasped low in its throat, and it leapt to the ground in one fluid movement. The instant its huge paws struck they propelled the albino cat forward along the valley. It did not look back, but long after it disappeared from sight the boy heard its growl from high above.

Fikizolo lay shivering for a long while, and he was honest enough to admit uncertainty as to whether it was from excitement or fear. But he did know one thing from the encounter.

The creature was the spirit of his dead father. He who was commander of the Leopard *iMpe* before he was born.

And now the white leopard watched over him, Fikizolo, who was also of the Leopard *iMpe*.

They reached the foothills of the Drakensberg at dusk, and the following morning the hunt for the white leopard began. The hunter ordered Fikizolo to search for spoor, for he had been told that the young warrior was a tracker of great ability.

All that day they climbed higher into the Berg, and it was late afternoon when Fikizolo found the leopard droppings.

He pointed to where its tracks led off to the right of the sheer cliffs above them.

But the white man was not fooled.

'Too small,' he growled. He spanned his hand over the four-toed print and its triangular pad, and shook his head. 'This is a female, and the one we want is male and twice the size. What does the tracker usually hunt? *Dassies?*'

His words were thrown contemptuously at Fikizolo, in the full knowledge that he was in the presence of his comrades of the Leopard *iMpe*. The young Zulu only stared at him, and did not reply. If the hunter had looked into the warrior's eyes at that moment, he would have seen the same look the great cats have - just before they make a kill.

That the white man would die before the hunt was ended, Fikizolo was certain. But not at his hand. The hunter was the king's friend, and whosoever laid angry hands on him would first have his eyes plucked out, then sharpened sticks forced up his nostrils into his brain, or driven into his anus.

Fikizolo continued to track for the rest of the day, but without success. Which was to be expected, for all the time he was moving away from the valley of the white leopard.

He knew it was there still, having seen it several times since his test of manhood. Yet, despite the reward, he would never betray it, for he had vowed then he would never hunt leopard, and would kill one only if his life was threatened.

This had brought a problem at the time of his testing, for there was no other fierce game that would be considered worthy of the initiate's spear.

Except, of course, for man.

His dilemma was resolved as he was returning, empty-handed, to the camp of the warriors who waited on the plains below.

He was attacked by two men of the *amaHlubi,* a tribe that dwelt to the north of *iNtabayikonjwa* - the mountain at which one must not point - and known to the whites as Giant's Castle. They had spent many days hunting unsuccessfully when they saw the youth, who bore the markings of the plains people to the east.

They ambushed him in a narrow cleft between the rocks, and when they moved in from both sides his doom appeared certain. Suddenly there came a warning growl from behind them, and the warriors of the amaHlubi made the fatal mistake of both looking at the same time.

Fikizolo's throwing spear flashed in the sunlight as it bit deeply into one man's chest, and before the other could move the youth had crossed the intervening space and struck upwards with his short stabbing spear, the Zulu's legacy from the days of Chaka.

The white leopard gave a coughing grunt, as though in approval for the boy's quick action, before melting back into the shadows of the rocks.

When Fikizolo dragged the bodies of the two full-grown warriors into the camp, the men of his tribe had slapped him on the back, accepting without question the trophies of his manhood test.

'What will you do if you kill the white beast, *Ndabandhlevu?*' he asked the white man at the fire that night. The grey-bearded hunter looked at him sharply, despite the politeness of his words.

For *Ndabandhlevu* meant, 'the beard that makes the law', and was a derisory nickname used by warriors in the service of the white man, due to his bossiness and insistence of being right in all things.

'WHEN I kill the white leopard,' he snapped. 'There is no IF about it. If you cannot find its spoor tomorrow you will return to the *kraal* of your king and explain to him why you have failed.'

The anger Fikizolo felt in his heart did not betray itself in his face, and the young black man did not speak further that night. Not even when the hunter described in detail how he would mount the beast's head on his wall, above the skin that he would strip from its back.

It was well past midnight when the roar came from the outer darkness, reverberating among the rocks and valleys of the Berg. Despite his years the white man was the first to his feet, fully clad and with rifle in hand. As though he had been lying awake - waiting for the white leopard to come to him.

'Fikizolo,' his roar matched the creature he sought, somewhere out there in the night. It was the first time he had called the young Zulu by name. 'Fetch a torch and find the beast. This is your last chance, boy.'

The anger that emanated from Fikizolo was shared by his friends of the *iMpe*. The indignity of referring to a proven warrior as 'boy' was a great insult, as it is has always been to the black people of America. But his friends were under the orders of the king, so he was on his own in dealing with the greybeard who thought his every word made it so by law.

They split up. A third of the party, including the cook and servants of the hunter, remained in the camp. Fikizolo led one of the hunting groups as tracker, and the other was by his comrade Zikhali. The white man went with Fikizolo.

At first he continued his previous ploy of guiding them away from the spoor of the albino, but the leopard had other intentions. He wanted them to follow, and Fikizolo obeyed his wishes. Steady roars and coughs drew the hunters higher into the peaks.

'We have him now,' the greybeard boasted. 'The devil's close. I can feel it in my bones. We have him.'

The young Zulu studied the tracks again, and smiled.

'One shot is all I ask for,' the man was voluble in his excitement. His dream of finishing a prolific career with a legendary kill was within his grasp. Perhaps it was that which stopped him from examining the tracks as well as he should.

As well as Fikizolo had done.

The young tracker had leaned down close to the patch of bare earth they had just passed over, and had seen a thing that he had never heard of, let alone seen, before. For the front part of each print was deeper in the soil than the pads, indicating that the pressure was placed on the toes first, and not the pad.

Which could only happen if the beast had walked backwards.

'This kill is mine,' the hunter snarled from behind the tracker. 'Mine alone. Wait for me here. Do not move from this spot. I order you.'

The warriors looked at each other as the greybeard dropped his rifle from the forearm carry and held it before him in readiness.

Fikizolo smiled at this waste of effort. He knew the leopard would take him from behind. Already he was stalking the greybeard from the high ground.

The Zulus sat around and spoke in low voices while they waited. Fikizolo knew they were nervous. He could tell the way they laughed too easily at the oft repeated stories of uTshwala - beer, Intombi - girls, and jabula - to rejoice. The universal soldiers' tall tales of wine, women and song.

'Thula,' he hissed suddenly. 'Be quiet. We are not the prey of the leopard this night.'

They all heard it then. The low coughing, followed by silence, then the sudden loudness of its growl as the creature sprang. In the ensuing struggle a shot was fired, an angry voice yelled in the language of the whites, then silence returned to the Berg as the night creatures paid homage to a fellow being, newly dead.

They found the hunter lying face down, between the boulders that had broken away from the cliffs and rolled down the slopes thousands of years before. Only when they turned him on his back did they see the dark gash where his throat had been ripped out.

A man was sent to fetch a blanket to wrap the body in, to be taken back to the king's *kraal* as proof of the manner in which he had died. While they waited the warriors of the Leopard *iMpe* faced outwards with their stabbing spears held in readiness.

Only Fikizolo, son of a commander of the Leopards, stood relaxed with his spear at his side. For he knew the white leopard had already made its kill for this night, as he had told his comrades earlier.

Never in his long life thereafter did he ever regret the loss of twice the bride-price he could have earned for leading the hunter to the valley of the white leopard.

When the great warrior died, he had been commander of the Leopard *iMpe* for the longest period of any man, and had been blessed with many fine sons from his beautiful, if fierce, wife.

And with the passing of Fikizolo, so too passed that other time.

The time of the animals.

During the next few days Joseph and Michael saw no fellow humans, or any sign of habitation. The weather was good at first, then rain dropped without warning on the second day, and they knew the northern drought was broken.

Michael was thankful for the raincoat he'd packed, and Joseph wrapped his blanket tightly around him. He politely refused the loan of the boy's coat, saying that his people used only blankets, for it was more important to be warm than dry.

On the third day they came to a *vlei* which would have been almost dry the week before. Now the deeper pools were filled and most of the *vlei* had a covering of water. The rain continued and they had to pick their way carefully across the firmer ground.

As often occurs, a large area had subsided, forming a big shallow lake, and Joseph led the way around the water. The blanket covered his head and his bag made a hump beneath it, causing the boy to smile at the sight. He loved the old man, and he'd never been happier than the past few days in his company.

He'd also loved his grandfather, of course, but it had been different with him. To the small boy he was a formidable figure; tall and stern - and totally unapproachable.

The rain stopped as suddenly as it had begun, and the sun shone with an intensity that caused a mist to rise, as the drying moisture rose and dissipated in the air above.

Michael's smile also dissipated as he heard the screams ahead. He looked at the old man but he was still walking along unconcernedly. Then the boy realised why. They were the delighted screams of children at play.

As they emerged from the thicker bush they saw a small group of black children playing at the water's edge. Two little girls, and their even smaller brother, splashed naked in the water.

The travellers paused for a while, taking the opportunity to remove their wet gear and hang it over bushes to dry. The children, absorbed in their pleasure at the sudden gift of water for their seemingly private use, did not notice them.

Joseph took out his pipe and began to fill it, smiling to himself at the happy sounds of childhood. The two girls came out of the water and without bothering to dry themselves, began to pull their dresses over their heads. Dresses that had been patched many times, probably handed down in the first place, but were clean and the little girls were obviously very proud of them as they pulled them down their boyish figures, while their girlish giggles rent the air.

A frown chased the smile from the boy's face as he became aware that something was terribly wrong. For the surface of the water was still, and there was no sign of...

'Joseph,' he cried. 'The little boy. He's gone.'

As the old man turned to look, the white boy ran past him and plunged into the water. Where he stood it only came to his knees, but when he moved out the bottom suddenly fell away, and he took a deep breath and dived into the hole.

The little girls began to scream in reality, and would have run back in the water if Joseph had not held them back. The white boy appeared, but he was alone. He took a deep breath and went down again.

After what seemed an eternity to the watchers, a small black head came up first, followed by Michael gasping for air. He pulled the boy out and laid him on his back.

He began mouth-to-mouth as the old man and the little girls watched silently. The still form suddenly began to cough, then choke, and his head turned to the side as water poured from his mouth. The lifesaver smiled up at the onlookers, then pumped the tiny chest. When he finally sat up, the two little girls ran forward and threw their arms around him.

'They are his sisters,' Joseph told the white boy, and he bent to pick up the child. 'They do not live far and they will lead us to their home.'

With the two little girls in front, Joseph holding the child in his arms and Michael dripping water, they made their way to the home of the children.

It was not far around the edge of the *vlei*, a small-holding consisting of a *rondavel* with a small brick hut to one side.

A dilapidated fence kept the few bedraggled fowl in the yard.

The mother was distressed when she saw her youngest child in the arms of a stranger, but Joseph spoke soothingly to her and she calmed down. He explained all that had happened, and was forced to repeat it a few minutes later when a man came hurrying in from the fields.

They insisted their son's rescuers stay for a meal, and Joseph told the boy it would be a rudeness to refuse. They were poor people, made poorer by the fortunes of farming in such an area, but they provided a good meal from what they had. A chicken was served, and by looking at the children's faces the old man knew it was not the usual fare. *Samp* - mealie meal and beans - was also on the table, with fresh mealie bread.

There was even a bottle of *iJuba* beer for Joseph.

They slept in the brick hut that night, and the children went into the *rondavel* with their parents. It was the first roof they'd been under for a week, and it felt strange to the boy.

The next morning breakfast was ready for the travellers before they continued their journey. Hot tea, mealie cakes, and boiled eggs. Once again they knew a small sacrifice had been made.

As they were leaving they thanked their hosts, and to his embarrassment the woman grasped hold of Michael's hand and kissed it. 'Thank...you, for saving our...child,' she said haltingly in English, and her husband shook his other hand in the Zulu way. The children gathered around, and it was some time before they could finally take their leave.

'Those people, Joseph,' the boy said after they'd been walking for a while. 'I feel so sorry for them. They have so little, yet they shared it all with us. They even killed one of their chickens.'

'Don't feel sorry for them, Michael,' the old man admonished. 'They are together as a family, with a roof over their heads and food on the table. It is more than many have in the world. They have also their pride, and by allowing them to give what they had, we left them that pride.'

The boy acknowledged the truth of this and fell silent.

When they stopped for lunch Joseph remarked on his continued, and unaccustomed, silence. Usually he was full of questions about the bush around them.

'I still feel bad about eating their food when they had so little,' he pulled his eyebrows together.

'They were Zulus and to them a debt must be repaid,' the old man said patiently. 'You saved the life of their only son, Michael, and to a warrior a son is the most important thing in his life. More so than a wife sometimes...'

His voice trailed off and the boy knew he was thinking of his own wife and son, and the different choice he had made.

'Anyway, Michael, if we do not get more food tomorrow, we will not have much ourselves.'

'The Zulu also repays anyone who has cheated him,' the boy said thoughtfully, not heeding the warning about food. 'My mother's father was a Boer, and had a sugar farm in northern Transvaal, a long time ago. It was near a big river that I can't remember the name of, but it was full of crocodiles. She told me a story once about the Zulu workers, and how they never got their pay one week, but they were quite happy about it.'

'That is indeed a story,' Joseph said solemnly, and he settled himself down against a fallen bluegum and began packing his pipe in anticipation. There is nothing a storyteller likes better than hearing someone else tell a tale.

'Are you sitting comfortably?' Michael teased. 'Then I will begin. Once upon a time...'

Joseph threw a small branch at him and they both laughed.

CHAPTER SEVEN

THE DEBT

'My grandfather was a good man to work for, and he always treated his men fairly,' Michael said seriously. 'They were always paid promptly when they'd finished work on a Friday, and they in turn gave him good value for money.

'One weekend a stranger came to the worker's *kraal* and began talking to them. He was a union official and he wanted them all to join his union. The people told him they were happy with the man they worked for, and that he paid them more than the unions were asking. But the man didn't want to listen to them and he made them scared by telling lies that they would all lose their jobs when the farm was closed down because they weren't in a union.

'So they joined, against the wishes of the *induna*, who said they should be loyal to my grandfather. They would not refuse to work, but the union man came up with the idea that they could go slow.

"Work to rule", he called it, and he told them it was done by White workers themselves, overseas.

'Starting on the Monday, they spent the week doing everything in slow motion, and when my grandfather wanted to know what was going on the *induna* told him. My grandfather pointed out that it was now time to cut the cane, and if they didn't bring it in before the rains came it would all be ruined.

'The union man stayed around to make sure that they kept to his orders. That week they did as much work as would normally have taken them a day, and my grandfather knew that if they kept it up he would lose everything.

'The man from the union knew that too.

'Friday came and the workers all lined up outside my grandfather's *stoep*. "What do you want?" he asked.

"Our money, *baas*," they replied.

"But you have worked very badly this week," he said. "Why should I pay you for doing less work than a dozen little girls could have done?"

"But you MUST pay us,' they said angrily. 'We have worked for you, now you must pay us. You cannot keep our money."

'The *induna* whispered to my grandfather that there would be much trouble if he didn't pay them, and my grandfather knew he was right. He also knew that he couldn't pay them or they would continue their go-slow and he would be ruined.

"Come at first light tomorrow, and I will have your money," he promised.'

Joseph was enjoying the story, and nodded slowly as he puffed away on his pipe.

'The next morning at dawn, all the workers were again lined up by the *stoep*, and my grandfather appeared with the *induna*. The *induna* carried the cash box, and without a word the two of them began to walk away from the house. The workers looked at each other with puzzled expressions, but they all followed behind.

'When they came to the river - the one I can't remember the name of - the *induna* put the cash box down and opened it. Each little brown envelope was filled with new rand coins, because the workers in those days did not recognise the value of paper money, and were suspicious of it.'

Again the grizzled head nodded and the old man chuckled, having a good idea where the story was going.

'My grandfather picked up the first pay envelope and called out the worker's name. As the man came forward to receive it, my grandfather flung it far out into the river, where it immediately sank to the bottom. The man stood blinking as the next name was called, and the same thing happened.

'The workers were amazed and did nothing as each name was called, and the money was thrown into the river. The crocodiles, alerted by the splashes and the number of people on the river bank, floated around looking like so many dead logs. But they fooled no one.

'Finally every man's name had been called and the money was all gone. The *induna* held the cash-box upside-down to prove it to them.

'Now I no longer have your money,' my uncle roared. 'But neither do you. If you want it, there it is.'

'He pointed to the river, where the crocodiles, angry at being disturbed as they were beginning to rest from their night's hunting, slashed the water viciously with their tails.

'Slowly the faces of the worker's began to change, and wide smiles broke out among them. Then they began to laugh, and soon they were rolling on the buffalo grass holding their sides, delighted at such a wonderful joke. For even though it was against themselves, they had to admire the cleverness of the white *baas*. He did not have the money, neither did they, and honour was satisfied all round.

'On the Monday they turned up for work as usual, and worked so hard that by the Friday they had made up for their slowness of the first week.'

'And the union man?' Joseph asked, for the black man likes to hear the details, and all loose ends must be cleared away.

'Never heard from again,' Michael grinned. 'They blamed him because they'd lost a week's pay, so they threw him into the river and told him to get it back. But I shouldn't think he succeeded.'

Joseph chewed on his pipe reflectively.

'No,' he said firmly. 'I shouldn't think he did.'

They burst out laughing. It wasn't the first time the old man had heard the tale, of course, but he was careful not to mention it to his young friend.

'That was a good story, *jong*,' Joseph said later, as they began to see signs of habitation. 'It is just as it would happen, I know. Your grandfather, he sounds like a wise man.'

'I wish I'd known him,' the boy said regretfully. 'He died when my mother was young, and the farm was sold. The family moved down to Durban, where my mother met my father.'

He sensed the hostility in the boy, and tried to appease him. 'Your English grandfather was a wise man too, Michael. He was a big man at the bank he worked at. Perhaps he was too stern at times, and perhaps that is why your father is also stern. But both were good men.'

'How can you say that, Joseph?' the boy cried. 'He was going to ship you off north in a small brick house where you don't know anyone, when the Berea has been your home for a long time.'

'More years than I can remember,' the old man said wistfully. 'But he is right. Because of my age I have become... what is the word?...a li...li...'

'Liability,' the boy said absently. 'But he's wrong. All you need is new glasses, then you'll be able to see all right, and everything will be fine again.'

'How can it be fine again after what we have done, Michael?' the old man said. 'We have both run off, and your father will blame me for leading you. Besides, I could never return to that life now. All I ask is that I can see the Barrier of Spears again before I die. Now, we are coming to a town I think, and we must be careful, my young friend.'

'Don't worry about money, Joseph,' the boy patted his back pack. 'I've got R600 that I drew out of the bank yesterday.'

'Then we have enough for food to take us to the western ocean if we want,' Joseph laughed. 'I too am well blessed.'

They approached the town from a line of heavy bush that merged with the shanty-town appearance of the Blacks and Coloureds dwellings. Originally small brick houses, government built and with nominal rent of a few rand per week, they had been added to over the years to provide extra accommodation for family members moving into the area from elsewhere. These additions consisted of demolition wood and tin roof sheeting.

Moving through the area was no problem. An old black man and a young white boy were not likely to draw AK47s on the people of the small township. Besides, according to Joseph, it was not a violent part of Natal.

Passing into the white part of town was like moving to another country. Like going from London during the *Blitzkrieg* to Washington D.C. The houses were vastly larger, well cared for, and with gardens that could have taken another few dwellings with ease.

They came to the main street, wide and clean looking, with all the usual shop signs in evidence. Pick 'n Pay, Clicks, CNA of course, and that odd assortment of butchers and smaller businesses.

At Michael's suggestion they selected a 7 Eleven store on the usual corner site, and approached it from the side street. By mutual consent it was left to Joseph to do the selective shopping, and the boy remained in the doorway.

He'd been there only a few minutes when he glanced across the road and saw a familiar figure striding along on the opposite side.

It was his father.

He stared, unable to believe his eyes at first, then realised they were in danger of being discovered. He dodged back into the store and found Joseph. The shopping expedition was abandoned, and they waited until the tall figure bent to open his car, then they dashed around the corner and back into the Blacks and Coloureds area.

Only when they were back in the bush once more did they slow down and pause to get their breath back. Joseph had to sit down for a while, and mopped his forehead with his handkerchief.

'You know, Michael,' he said finally. 'This could be your chance to go home if you want to. It is not me your father is looking for, and I think his joy would be such that he would not punish you.'

'No,' the boy glared at him. 'We started this together and we'll finish it together. If I gave in now I'd never get the chance to climb in the Drakensberg.'

The old man climbed wearily to his feet, but managed a small smile as they began to walk again.

They stopped in the late afternoon, and Joseph busied himself in the bush nearby while Michael, experienced now in bivouac building, prepared their camp for the night.

When the old man finally returned, he was carrying a crude bow and some arrows. Michael had a small fire going, and the tips of the arrows were pushed into the flames to fire-harden them.

'My people learned the art of bow-making from the Bushmen, many years ago,' the old man explained, as he tested each arrow in turn. 'It was handed down through father to son, and as a young man I would hunt with them. Do not worry about supper, Michael. If I cannot get something with the bow then perhaps the snares I've laid will do better.'

The mention of supper made the boy realise they'd eaten nothing since the morning, when they'd shared his last chocolate bar. As he watched the old man stroll off to check his traps, he hoped fervently that he would be lucky.

He had the tea brewing by the time Joseph returned, holding two guinea-fowl aloft in triumph.

'We will eat well tonight, Michael,' he grinned.

They did indeed. Both were roasted over the fire, and they did full justice to the succulent birds. What remained was wrapped in leaves to take with them the next day.

'The bow and arrows, Joseph,' the boy said later, as they relaxed by the fire and the old man was drawing deeply on his pipe. 'There must be a lot that you can remember of the old days.'

'Oh, yes, *jong*. I remember much. The *intombis* - maidens - dancing in the village. Their beads would be flapping wildly as they kicked high and thumped their feet down with the power of the elephant. Screaming old women would scoot to and fro with grass brooms to keep the girls in line.'

He paused to reflect.

'They were beautiful, those girls. They wore only short skirts to cover their maidenhood, and their bare breasts would jut out proudly, glistening with the oils they rubbed on them. The matrons wore long leather skirts, and tall maroon-ochured hairstyles, and most of them wished they could be maidens again.'

His eyes closed as he remembered the days of his youth.

'And the warriors. They were tall and strong, wearing back panels of calf skin, animal skin sporrans, and side tails to mark their position as blooded warriors. Some wore the Zulu headrings, which were built into their hair, for that was the tradition. They would sit around on their haunches, playing the game of *iMpes*, or the warrior game, on the hard dung floor of the huts. The "warriors" were bubbles blown through reeds, after they'd puffed at the *ingudu* bubble pipes. These were filled with *dagga* - hemp - which was legal in those days but only the privilege of the older men. We boys would sit and watch them, pointing out the heroes and the great hunters, and vowing to be like them when we grew older.'

He sighed again for times past, and the pipe lay on the ground by his side now, forgotten for the moment.

'But by the time we were men, everything had changed. The Whites had become more numerous than the blades of grass on the *veldt*, and their way of life had taken over from ours.'

He appeared to be speaking to himself now, for often he would lapse into Zulu, though the boy was still able to understand most of his words.

'Instead of hunting the plains and the mountains as a warrior, I have spent many years of my life doing the work of a woman. But I cannot find it in my heart to blame the Whites. As well blame the Black for allowing himself to accept the white culture. His electricity, his modern toys, and his vices. We are all to blame, Michael, not just the Whites.'

'But didn't the Boers do some awful things to the black people, in the old days?'

'Yes, but no worse than the British did to the Boer when they fought each other. Many thousands of Afrikaners died in the prison camps of the British; men, women and children. There was a man once, a black man, who might have been able to bring peace and understanding to our land, but his understanding and goodness made them afraid, and they killed him.'

'Like Jesus,' the boy murmured.

'Like Jesus,' the grey head nodded. 'There is a saying in your language, that what a fool does not understand he destroys. I'm afraid it is true.'

'This man you talk about, was he a great chief, like Chaka?'

'No,' the old man began to refill his pipe, a sure sign that another tale was about to unfold. 'He was just a blacksmith.'

CHAPTER EIGHT

THE BLACKSMITH

The wind began gently at first, the old man said in his own way, plucking at the corners of the Union Jack which draped the coffin, and ruffling the garments of the more than 3,000 mourners.

Perhaps the wind realised its efforts were not enough to disturb such a multitude, for it increased its intensity and a sudden and violent thunderstorm began. The British flag was torn to pieces by the rushing wind, and before the coffin was lowered hastily into the waiting earth, the terrified mourners were stumbling away with their hands making the sign of the cross. For they were reminded of another burial and another storm, some 2,000 years before. Prayers fell unbidden from their lips.

By his death this man had also become a martyr, and that violent storm on the day of his burial turned him into a legend among his people.

During the time of the Boer War, and even after the signing of the peace treaty on the 31 May, 1902, commandos rode out of the Boer republics of the Transvaal and the Orange Free State, and fought across the rest of South Africa.

One of the daring young leaders was a man named Gideon Scheepers, who when finally caught by the British, was executed in a somewhat shameful manner at Graaf-Reinet. He has now taken his place in history as an Afrikaner martyr, and rightly so, for there was no glory to the British that day.

But bad deeds are committed on both sides in the name of causes, and a year earlier had seen an even worse death happen to another leader. A black man named Abraham Esau.

Abraham was born in 1855 at Kenhardt in Bushmanland, where he was the eldest child of Adam Esau and Martha April. His parents had been deeply influenced by Wesleyan missionaries, from whom they had gained a basic education.

Often they spoke English at home, a practice as unusual now as it was then. Abraham was educated at an English church school in Prieska, and was much impressed by the language and culture of the English. The Bible became his way of life.

In 1880 he moved to Calvinia, a small town to the north of Cape Town. He became a blacksmith, and by dint of hard work he built his own smithy, as well as growing and selling vegetables.

Although the Cape Colony was governed by the British, the people who lived there consisted of both Afrikaners and English, and the rebel Boers on their frequent incursions into the colony found many supporters among the Afrikaners. In many districts, the laws of the Boers concerning 'traditional native policies', were administered by local rebels, and they handed out swift justice to any African who disobeyed these 'laws'.

Many were forced to serve the invading rebels, or to work on white-owned farms, usually for little or no payment. Black produce and stock were often seized without requisition chits being handed over for future compensation. Many Coloureds or Africans held the franchise to their land, and they asked the government for weapons with which to protect themselves and their property. Because the Cape Afrikaners protested against this, even threatening to join the rebels officially, the government turned down their request.

This was the situation on the 19 May 1900, when celebrations to commemorate the relief of Mafeking were held in the town.

Abraham Esau, now a man of some prominence in Calvinia, had organised it all. There were speeches in the market square by both the magistrate and Abraham himself. When he raised the union Jack, it was publicly acknowledged that he was now the leader of the Coloured community. As such he began to form a militia company to protect the town against invasion from the republican Boers. He wrote to both the magistrate and British intelligence agent at Clanwilliam, suggesting that a native levy be formed.

The magistrate refused, being worried about an Afrikaner mutiny if this were to come about, and although the intelligence agent agreed that it would be an excellent idea, he was only a mere lieutenant and did not have the authority to sanction it.

Undaunted, Abraham went ahead and organised not so much an army as a highly effective intelligence network, covering a large area of the northern Cape. When word of this 'poisonous Hottentot in Calvinia', reached the Boers they were determined to punish him.

Early on the morning of the 10 January, 1901, a *Kommando* from the free State, reinforced with Cape rebels, attacked the little town. Led by the blacksmith, the unarmed Coloured people resisted the invaders with only sticks and stones. The outcome was inevitable, with a number being shot down and the rest savagely beaten. Abraham and the local officials were thrown into jail.

The Boer rebels were led by Commandant Charles Niewoudt, who then forced the population into the market square, where he proclaimed himself the new magistrate.

He also proclaimed that the laws of the Republics would apply, especially in regard to 'Hottentots and Kaffirs'.

They were to pay tax or come forward for labour, and were forbidden from speaking English in public.

Every infringement of the Boer laws brought severe punishment, including being outdoors after curfew, gatherings of two or more people, failing to have a pass, or disturbing the peace. The latter meant the singing of patriotic British songs.

Local Afrikaner farmers began bringing in their 'insubordinate or troublesome' labourers for correction, and a local paper, The Diamond Fields Advertiser, reported that 'every Dutchman in the district who had a grudge against his employees brought them before the *Landdrost'*. More than 100 labourers were brought in to be beaten, subjected to hard labour, or have their children taken away to serve in the Commandos as 'apprentices'.

For every supposed offence, Abraham Esau was held to blame.

They said his influence on the black community, and his arrogance in refusing to renounce his allegiance to Britain, had caused them to commit their 'crimes'. Nightly, his supporters marched through the streets in defiance of the curfew, chanting his name and singing hymns.

Furious now, Niewoudt had Abraham dragged from the jail, beaten, smeared with dung and offal, and left chained to a pole in the intense heat of the midday sun. Children brought him water, and at one time nearly a hundred of his supporters confronted the Boers, but Abraham begged them to leave, not wanting any more of his people to suffer.

The next day he was dragged before the Boer commander and sentenced to 25 lashes, 'for having spoken against the Boers and for having attempted to arm the natives'.

Abraham was tied to a tree and Niewoudt himself decided to apply the lashes. When at last he finished, the prisoner was untied and collapsed to the ground, where he was repeatedly kicked. At last he was dragged away unconscious. Throughout the next two weeks he was lashed and beaten, and on one occasion he was even stoned by the men of Niewoudt's Kommando.

Finally, on the 5th February, his misery ended. He was placed in leg irons, tied between two horses and dragged a few kilometres out of town. There he was shot in the back.

The Cape pro-Boer newspapers would justify his death by saying that Abraham Esau had been shot 'in self-defence', while a British newspaper made the summation that, 'he has suffered cruel martyrdom for no worse crime than loyalty to the British'.'

History would show that their loyalty to the British would cost the African dearly in the end. Although none were on the official roll calls of either army, it is now estimated that as many as 100,000 served both British and Boer as labourers, drivers, guides, etc., and by the end of the war nearly 10,000 Africans were serving under arms in the British forces.

The Boers flogged or shot many of the non-combatants, and in Mafeking nearly 2,000 of the African garrison were shot by the Boers; or left to die of starvation by Baden-Powell. In the end it was the Africans who had to pay the heaviest price of the war, both during and after.

For no matter which side won, the black people could gain nothing themselves.

The final irony is not just the senseless death of Abraham, but the tragic loss of an educated man. For as a leader and visionary, this blacksmith could have brought all of his skills together to help forge the understanding and ability to communicate that, sadly, has still not been resolved to the present time.

Today, if you drive out of Calvinia, west on the R27, you won't travel very far before you come to a little dorp named Nieuwoudtville.

But search as you will, you will not find an Esauville.

There were tears in the boy's eyes when Joseph finished his story, and the old man nodded in understanding, and strangely, a measure of satisfaction. For it was further confirmation of the caring that was in the heart of the grandson of the old *baas*.

The next morning the old man was gone before Michael stirred. He blew the fire back into life and added the slow build-up of kindling and wood as he'd been shown. By the time Joseph came back the fire was ready for cooking, which was just as well, for the old warrior held up a *dassie* as proof that his snares were good.

They ate most of it, and though at first the boy had an aversion to eating one of the cute little creatures, hunger won out in the end.

They began their journey that day with full stomachs, not knowing if there would be much for supper, yet somehow not caring one way or the other. They had the remains of the guinea-fowl and the *dassie*, and they would not starve before morning.

In the afternoon Joseph stopped suddenly and raised his head to sniff the air. He gazed ahead without seeing.

'I smell *uKhahlamba*, and I think I can see it now.'

Michael peered ahead but could see nothing. One thing he had learned was patience, and he proved it now while he waited for the old man to continue walking.

An hour later he looked up, and there in the distance was the Drakensberg. The Barrier of Spears that he'd waited to see for so long.

Yet not as long as his companion on the journey.

That night he asked the old man how the Bushman came to live in the mountains of the Drakensberg before the Bantu, and why they now chose to live in the inhospitable deserts of the Khalahari and the Namib.

'It was not by choice, Michael,' Joseph replied, sucking on his old pipe. 'We have eaten early tonight, so perhaps there is time to tell you of the early Bushman and of what happened to the last ones, for it is a long story.'

CHAPTER NINE

THE HUNT

During their long migratory journey down the length of the African continent, the small bands of the tribe who called themselves *San* were attacked by the various peoples of the lands they travelled through.

To these they were known by the derisory term, Bushmen.

When they finally ran out of land and saw only the Indian Ocean before them, they knew they could go no further, for here there was no great drift of land like the one previous generations had crossed to the continent of Africa from Europe. They decided to stay where they were, and survive as best they could.

At first it was all that they wanted and they lived as part of the land they venerated, and the game was plentiful. Then came the black men, and some made their peace with the little people. They saw they were not a threat, for they did not cultivate the ground nor graze cattle upon it, and took only the game they needed.

Nor did they wage war on other tribes; unlike the Blacks who came after, killing and burning the *kraals* of their fellows, and driving off their cattle. They did not try to understand the Bushman and hunted him down, for no other reason than he was there.

Then came the white man with his modern weapons that spat death faster than the Bushman could draw his bow, and he too joined in the slaughter. For centuries the taller races of Southern Africa, Black and White, attempted to wipe out the little people, and in this they finally succeeded.

For today no Bushmen exist in the Drakensberg.

As the 1800s moved towards the final decades, the mark of the white settlers had already been stamped on the plains to the east of the ranges and the lower valleys of the Drakensberg. Game had become scarce for the remaining Bushmen, although in summer they moved to the highlands where the rains had caused the sweet new grass to grow, and this in turn would attract antelope to feed.

It was in the winter that food became a problem for the little people, though seldom a threat to survival, for they could find sustenance everywhere. Choice venison was their favourite, but when they descended from the high places it was to find a scarcity of game.

The settler could hunt easily here, and with his horse and rifle nothing that lived in the *bushveldt* could elude him.

Unlike the Bushman, the Whites killed much more than they needed. They killed for the horns of the *kudu* and the skin of the *elandt*. Sadly, not for the meat to feed their families.

Gian was the leader of a small band who made their home in the mountains, and no-one could say how long they'd been there. Not even his own father's father, who was the oldest man Gian had ever known, and who told tales of their ancestors crossing a great river on a stretch of land that spanned two continents.

Well over a century later, the white man with his magic would be able to make an accurate guess that it was three thousand years before the birth of Christ that Gian's forebears first gazed up at the towering peaks of the then nameless mountains.

To his ultimate detriment, he decided to stay.

The sun was devoid of the intense heat of the summer yet still shone down with a pleasant warmth. The nearby waters of the Sterkspruit were freezing in contrast, having come swiftly down from the melting snows on the top.

Gian and his three companions had just finished a successful hunt, and were squatting around the carcass of a *blesbok*, an animal soon to become extinct in the area, for the Whites had also discovered the excellent quality of its meat.

The hunters had gutted the *blesbok* and were eating the warm liver and kidneys to give them strength for the trek back to the home cave with their prize. It had not been easy, for while they were slowly stalking their prey Gian's young son, Oba, had become over confident on this his first hunt, and loosed an arrow too soon.

The buck had been off like that arrow, similar to the one in Gian's bow which he had been in the act of drawing when the sound startled it. So began a race for the life of the animal. The *blesbok* to keep it, and the Bushmen to take it.

The antelope's head was further from the ground than the hunters yet they matched it stride for stride, gradually beginning to catch up to it. Young Oba, who did not have the older men's stamina yet still possessed the speed of youth, began to draw away. It was his fault the buck had taken off before his father could fire the fatal arrow, and which would have meant a leisurely track until they came across the dead beast.

Now, because of him, it had turned into a race, and it was incumbent upon him to atone for that by making the kill himself. Not that the others would pull back and allow him to, for there was no time for indulging the mistakes of the young in the Bushman's world. The kill was the only thing that mattered.

For all their sakes.

Taking an arrow from its wooden quiver, and holding it loosely in the bow, he burst forward alongside the back legs of the *blesbok*. Oba knew that he would not be able to continue the pace for long, and his first arrow had to find its target. At the same time he had to avoid the deadly tip as he drew back the bow, still keeping his legs pumping to match the speed of the frightened animal.

The arrow struck the flank of the *blesbok* and bit deep, the main shaft falling away on impact, and the poison slowly began to take effect.

The hunters slowed down to a fast jog, knowing it would not be long before the stricken beast collapsed. By the slight nod of his father's head, and the grunts of the two others, he knew he had made up for his previous carelessness. Oba, barely twelve years of age, was content.

When the meal was finished the animal was bound to a pole and carried by the two warriors while the father and son walked on ahead, not communicating but each with his own sense of pride, reliving the hunt in their minds.

The others had already put the hunt behind them and were thinking ahead to the night's feasting and celebration, for it was nearly two weeks since they had tasted meat. They would roast it over the cooking fire and it would be supplemented by roots and berries, and whatever else the women had been skilled, and lucky enough, to find.

The man in front, Raan, was hoping they'd found some nests so they could have what the blacks called 'Bushman's rice', the chrysalis of ants or termites eggs roasted with rich animal fats in a baked earthenware pot. He also dreamed of honey, but the chance of the women finding some in that season was remote.

Xinob, on the other hand, was not thinking of food at all, but rather of the music they would have that night. In his mind the food was already eaten, and washed down with several mouthfuls of the intoxicating honey drink the women brewed.

He was the best musician in the little band and only the night before the hunt he had finished his new drum. It had taken Xinob's woman a long time to cure the small skin of a grey *duiker*, which he had then stretched over the neck of a clay pot and bound tightly with animal sinew. Xinob could hardly restrain himself from dropping his end of the pole and sprinting for the cave to play it.

So they wended their way towards the high peaks of the Drakensberg, and the home cave. Each with his own thoughts, yet collectively covering all that the little people wanted from life. The hunt, food, music; and the most important of all. Pride.

Some twenty kilometres behind and to the east of the Bushmen, six white men were eating a cold lunch by the banks of the Sterkspruit.

Only the food was cold, for the contents of the bottle they passed back and forth contained a brandy that seemed brewed from fire, so fierce was its bite. It was the second bottle they'd consumed since stopping over an hour before.

The hunters had followed the river from a small trading *dorp* that would one day be known as the town of Winterton, following the bloody war between the Whites that would soon be upon them. The men were on a hunting trip, an indulgence they allowed themselves every few weeks.

They could well afford to, for they were wealthy, self-made men who had wrested more than a good living from the land, yet not to the good of the land. The exception was Pieter Koorts, the son of Tiaan Koorts who owned one of the largest farms in the area.

They were as different, father and son, as the mighty water buffalo is from the graceful *oribi* and the comparison was not unreasonable. Koorts senior was a huge man, with a neck that began below his ears and sloped straight down to the point of his shoulders, while his son was shorter and half his father's breadth. His hair was much fairer, and his features almost too handsome, giving an air of fragility that his father despised. He possessed a gentleness and love of knowledge that his father also held in contempt.

'Tiaan,' Johann Malan tossed the bottle over to the older Koorts, who was frowning slightly at his son, propped against a rock reading a small book. Malan came from Huguenot stock and owned the largest store in the town, his wealth coming mainly from the enormous trade in skins and horns. In his spare time he would hunt, thereby saving payment at the going rate of a shilling a hide.

The other farmer, Stoffel van Wyk, was the oldest of the group, being close to sixty-five years, and his three sons now did all of the work on the farm, thus enabling him to get away on his hunting trips. Like his friend Tiaan, Stoffel van Wyk ruled his family, as he did his *kaffir* herdsmen. With a rod of iron.

Willie Styger was the size of the older Koorts, but a large proportion of his bulk was fat. As a young man in his native Germany, Styger had been a woodsman like his father before him, yet had inherited none of that love of the forest his sire had possessed. On the contrary, he was the first to combine the individual woodcutters of the area into a single lumber business, and direct them after the trees in a voracious fashion.

Yellowwoods, black ironwoods, Cape chestnuts, stinkwood; none were safe from the axes and saws of his men, despite the distances they had to travel to acquire them. Although the mid-fifties had seen the introduction of permits to cut timber, men like Willie Styger ignored them, and had grown rich denuding the forests of the plains and the foothills of the Drakensberg.

The last member of the party, stretching his long arm out in leisurely fashion for the brandy bottle, was an Englishman named Jolyon Prentice-Smythe. He was a man in his late forties and of independent means, for he had no established business nor apparent means of income. The rumour that he was the younger son of a wealthy member of the aristocracy, unable to succeed to the title and therefore sent to the Colonies with a handsome allowance, was well known to everyone.

And so it should, for Jolyon (born Herbert Smith in Battersea) had spent some time on its circulation, and his generous entertaining of the local burghers had served to enhance the story. His money had initially come from embezzling his employer in London, from where he took ship to Africa under his new name, then investing in the slave trade in Mocambique.

There we leave the hunting party; one nice young man who would rather be a scholar than a hunter, and five not-so-nice older men who had few limitations when it came to money or sport. Thus far on the trip the latter had eluded them, but they were to make up for it over the next few days.

A few days were exactly the time it would take Gian and his companions to get home. They made good speed on the first day, and built a fire beneath a giant protea, over which they roasted a haunch of the *blesbok* and amply filled their bellies. They slept on the ground as always, pulling their cloaks of *dassie* fur about them to stave off the cold.

At first light they fed on raw meat, then moved on once more, a few clicks from the leader being the only conversation between them. After an hour's travel the mist lifted in the distance and the mountains came into view, whereupon each hunter felt an uplifting of the spirit and gave silent praise, each in his own way.

Towards noon they turned towards the river so they could drink from its refreshing waters, when Gian, on the rear of the pole and therefore the last man, stopped suddenly.

He grunted to the others and they stood as still as the distant peaks, heads held high, listening.

Finally the leader knelt, turned his head to the side and placed an ear to the ground. He arose and nodded, having no need to speak. All were now aware that something was behind, and although many kilometres back it was travelling fast and would soon be upon them.

The six hunters had come across the scene of the Bushman kill just before last light, and their experience on the *veldt* told them exactly what it was, and who had been there.

Not long after lunch Malan had shot a pair of plump guinea-fowl and they made an early camp, dining well off the tasty flesh of the birds, washed down with brandy from their seemingly endless supply.

'Drink, Pieter,' his father thrust the bottle towards him.

'No, thank you, *vader*,' the young man looked up from the book he was reading by the firelight. 'I do not care for it.'

'He does not care for it,' Koorts mimicked. He had already drunk well, and his temper did not improve with quantity. 'Bah, the boy is useless. He doesn't care for brandy, the same way he doesn't care for hunting or farming. My only son and he acts more like a *verdompde* daughter.'

His big hand reached out and snatched the book. It was small and bound in green leather. The words IN MEMORIAM and TENNYSON were etched in gold on the spine. He riffled through the pages and his face took on a livid aspect.

'Poetry,' he spat, as though it was a dirty word. 'And not just poetry but *verdompde* English poetry.'

With a snarl he flung the handsomely bound book into the fire, where at first the flames seemed to recede from it, as though they too were appalled at the act of desecration taking place. Then greed overcame them, and they closed in and licked hungrily at the curling pages.

The men looked at the young man; some with amusement, others with curiosity. Not one expression showed even a hint of sympathy.

He disappointed them all, and merely shook his head and gazed at the spot where his book had become only a fiery outline, and his lips moved as though he was forgiving the fire for its part in his loss.

'The stars', she whispers, 'blindly run;

A web is wov'n across the sky;

From out waste places comes a cry,

And murmurs from the dying sun;

And all the phantom,

Nature, stands...'

'Enough,' his father roared, swaying dangerously above him. 'Enough of this English shit...' the hand holding the bottle rose into the air, as though he intended to bring it down on his son's head.

'*Dankie*,' Stoffel van Wyk held out his hand. 'Give me another drink of that, Tiaan, before you do something very wasteful with it, *meneer*.'

His companions roared with laughter, and the situation was diffused as Koorts shoved the bottle into the older man's hand and snorted off into the darkness to relieve the pressure on his bladder.

'You shouldn't be unkind to the damn English, either,' Johann Malan called out to the blackness beyond the fireglow. 'If it weren't for our aristocratic friend here we wouldn't have all this brandy you've been downing. He's not mean like some.'

They all laughed again, the Englishman especially. Koorts was well known for being 'careful'. An answering burst of laughter came from the darkness, for meanness WAS something he was proud of.

The only one who did not join in the laughter was young Pieter, still staring fixedly into the fire. He was seeing things the others would never be aware of, even if they had the eyes to see.

By the time they crawled out of their blankets the next morning, the Bushmen had been travelling for many hours. The brandy of the night before and the coldness of the dawn had kept the hunters to their beds longer than intended.

Pieter had already revived the fire and had tea made and breakfast on the way. It was over heaped plates of *boerewors* and beans, washed down with strong hot tea, that plans for the day were made.

'We must head for the mountains and hunt up the valleys at this time of year,' Malan said, and the others nodded in agreement.

'Maybe we can have some sport on the way, *ja?*' the German said, tearing a large piece of sausage with discoloured teeth.

'How so?' asked the man who called himself Prentice-Smythe.

'He means the kill we found back there,' the older Koorts had inclined his head in the direction they'd come. 'The spoor led this way.'

'Oh, you mean chase those little cavemen chappies,' the Englishman had no problem holding to his upper class accent. It had been difficult at first, before he realised the Boers knew no different. 'What a splendid idea.'

'You can't mean hunt them down like jackals?' the young man's face held a whiteness that owed nothing to the coldness of the morning. 'That would be murder. *Vader*, you couldn't...'

'Rubbish, boy,' the older Koorts snapped. 'The little *boggers* have raided White farms and taken their cattle.'

'But only because they were hungry,' Pieter cried. 'We have killed off most of the game they always lived off. Even so, they take only the odd cow here and there.'

'It is the odd cow too much, lad,' growled van Wyk. 'It is upon us to get rid of them whenever we have the opportunity, and we have been given that now,'

'*Ja*,' agreed the destroyer of forests, wiping a sleeve across his greasy lips. 'I agree.'

'Why the devil not?' the Englishman gained his feet eagerly. 'Let's go hunting, gentlemen.'

The Bushman's ability to see long distances was uncanny, and was matched only by his acute sense of hearing.

By the time the horsemen reached the place where they were, the little men had disappeared. Gian had become a tree stump, Raan a rock, and Xinob an extra branch of a dense protea. Oba had slipped into a fold of ground between his father and the river. The buck had been buried, in such a way that only a man searching slowly on foot would have a chance of discovering it.

So well had the Bushmen become part of the landscape around them that the hunters galloped right past. They were no longer tracking the spoor, for they knew well where the little men were heading.

They were two hundred metres past the spot when two things happened at once. Tiaan Koorts glanced back over his shoulder, and at the same time the boy, Oba, incautiously raised his peppercorn head above the ground.

With a whoop of satisfaction the heavy Boer turned his horse at the gallop and rode straight for the spot where he'd seen the young Bushman. As he heard the thunder of the hooves bearing down on him, Oba took to his heels and ran towards the river. With the speed of desperation, combined with his natural ability, he would probably have made it.

Except this was not the first time the big Afrikaner farmer had hunted Bushmen, and he had seen them outrun horses before. He reined his mount in hard and pulled his rifle from its saddle scabbard.

He tucked the butt into his shoulder, adjusted the rear sight and took his time aiming. His first shot was just on the heels of the fleeing Bushman, and kicked up dirt and stones against the terrified boy's legs.

His second shot was even closer and landed between the young Bushman's feet.

'Enough, Tiaan,' shouted the bearded Malan. 'Get it over with, man.'

The third shot did just that, ploughing into his back to the left of the spine and bursting through his heart to lodge in his breast bone. The force of the heavy piece of lead drove him forward another six metres before he collapsed into a pathetically small heap on the ground.

The rest of the party had walked their horses back, Pieter protesting and the others howling their appreciation of the shot.

Of the six horsemen, only Stoffel van Wyk did not view the kill.

He was farthest away and he did not see the rock behind him turn into a Bushman and nor did he sense his own death until the arrow took him in the side of the throat. He slipped from his horse and was dead before he hit the ground, his life blood pumping out in great gouts from the severed jugular.

The poison on the tip was unnecessary.

As soon as he had released his arrow, Raan had turned and kicked up his heels. It was possible he could outdistance the horses and if he led them far enough away his two remaining companions could retrieve the buck and take it to their hungry ones. If he did not do this then the Whites would comb the area until they found and killed them all.

Raan had come across the fair skinned ones before, and he knew them to be tenacious and thorough when the fever of the hunt was upon them.

Malan turned his head at the sound of the heavy body hitting the ground, and saw the little killer running swiftly off across the *veldt*. With hardly a glance at his stricken companion, he dug his heels into the flanks of his mount and charged after the Bushman. The Englishman took off after him with a cry he'd heard at the local hunts in the land of his birth.

Pieter Koorts was the only one to go to the aid of the old farmer, and he could do no more than close the eyes and straighten his limbs. By the time he'd done this Malan and Prentice-Smythe had flanked Raan and were loosing off shots from the saddle.

Luck more than skill was attributable to the bullet that struck the Bushman in his right thigh, passing cleanly through without striking bone but causing great blood loss.

Weakening now, and realising the inevitability of his situation, Raan finally stopped and turned to face his pursuers, and already he was nocking an arrow to his bow as they bore down on him.

He could feel his strength ebbing from him as the blood ran down his leg to form a dark pool at his feet. Even then Raan could think of the land, and he was pleased that his life fluids would not be wasted but would be absorbed, and so help to sustain the land.

His first arrow dropped by half a metre and took Malan's horse in the left eye. It went down on its knees, throwing the rider forward over its neck. As his mount was dying, the trader was already rolling to his feet and firing his long barrelled pistol at the run. One of the bullets ripped into Raan's shoulder, causing his second arrow to fly wildly into the storm clouded sky. Another piece of lead tore away his left kneecap and he fell to the ground.

The Englishman reined hard and leapt from his horse before it had stopped, the momentum pushing him forward until he was almost on top of the little man with the yellowish brown skin. As he stood over him in triumph, struggling to get his pistol out of its cumbersome side holster for the *coup de grace*, the Bushman moved suddenly.

To the surprised white man the figure that rose before him appeared to take on huge proportions, and the red tinged eyes seemed level with his own.

While he stared hypnotically into them, a stone knife of the kind used 50,000 years before thrust upwards. The crude weapon glanced off his ribs and ripped away a large piece of flesh and muscle.

The sudden pain shook the Englishman from his trance and he went into a berserk rage. His pistol was drawn and he pumped shots into the small figure. When the chamber was empty he held the weapon by the barrel and pounded the heavy grip into the unresisting face of the dead Bushman.

Only the tight hands on his shoulders brought him back to the present, and the pain in his side. He absently pulled his torn shirt over the gaping hole in his flesh and held it in place.

'You can stop now, Jolyon,' Malan spoke in his ear. 'I think you have killed the little *bogger* six times already.'

They found an abandoned ant-bear hole and slipped the body of the old Boer down it, filling the top few feet with rocks to keep hyenas and other scavengers away. Malan took over his horse and they left van Wyk's saddle and possessions in a cache nearby, intending to pick them up on the way back. Prentice-Smythe's wound had been attended to and the group got under way again.

'We'll go on to the caves where these dirty little animals hide,' the older Koorts had declared when they'd said a few words from the good book over their friend Stoffel. 'And we'll exterminate them once and for all.'

No one opposed this and they mounted up and rode towards the mountains. The bodies of the two little Bushmen were left where they fell, and only Pieter Koorts looked back with a small prayer on his lips.

For a moment he thought he saw two little figures standing where the bodies lay, but he knew it was only a trick of the light, and his imagination.

It was neither the light nor his imagination that the young Boer had seen, for Gian and Raan were paying homage to their dead before quickly burying them in shallow graves scraped out with their digging sticks. The meat was forgotten, for it no longer had the same importance than before the white hunters had appeared.

The Bushman lived by certain codes of ethics, and although he had never seen a bible, an eye for an eye would have appealed to him, for do unto others was his way of life. The Whites had invaded his hunting lands and killed his game, and so the little men had descended the valleys, crossed the plains, and killed the white man's cattle.

When a Bushman was killed by Black or White, reprisals were made.

Now the son of Gian and the friend of Xinob had been killed, shot down like the scavenger dogs of the *veldt*, and Whites would die in consequence. Many generations later the Bushman would decide that the continuance of the tribe was the paramount concern, and the word 'revenge' passed out of their language forever.

As the burghers entered the foothills of the Dragon Mountains, known to the Zulu as *Quathlamba*, the Barrier of Spears, the little men they sought were not far behind them.

For the hunted had become the hunters.

The mood at the fire that night was not good. Tiaan Koorts was in his cups early, talking loudly. Of a sudden, Stoffel van Wyk was the greatest man who had ever lived, and Tiaan's closest friend.

Willie Styger sipped his brandy slowly and thought of the next day with a mixture of apprehension and excitement. Despite his words he did not like to be in Bushman country at night, for he knew just how deadly the little men could be. Yet he had killed them before, and given half the chance would do so again.

His excitement came from the thought of the girls he'd find up there. His taste for young flesh was hard to satisfy, living as he did amongst Dutch Calvinists. His appetite had been confined to the children of poor Blacks, who for a small sum would see nothing.

The Englishman's wound had worsened during the day and he was now lying in his blankets before the fire, moaning and muttering to himself. They had poured brandy down his throat and wrapped him well, but none gave much for his chances.

The fire was stoked up well and each man stood watch in turn. Pieter drew the five o'clock shift and found the man he was to relieve, Styger, fast asleep near the fire. He could feel something wrong, but could not fathom what it was. He quietly examined each of the blanket wrapped men, and much to his relief found they all slept soundly, evidenced by their snores and the feverish mutterings of the Englishman.

Then he realised what gave him the feeling of unease.

The absence of night noises.

Outside the camp area there should have been the small sounds of nocturnal creatures hunting. The hoot of an owl, perhaps the cough of a cheetah or leopard, or the maniacal cackle of a hyena when it finds something to eat.

And the snuffling and stamping of the horses, the rubbing sounds of their head ropes and ground hobbles.

Instead there was nothing.

The night was as silent as the tops of the peaks on a still day in summer. Pieter thought of waking his father but remembered the angry response when shaken from a drunken slumber. Instead, despite his feeling of trepidation he picked up his rifle and went alone to investigate the picket line.

As he approached silently in the darkness, his eyes ruined by the fireglow, his feet struck something and he fell forward, his knees sinking into a large object that gave slightly under his weight. He reached out a hand and felt the still warm coat.

Without caring for his own safety Pieter stumbled back to the fire, pulled out a burning branch and hurried back. The blazing torch revealed a scene of horror to the young man.

The five horses were lying on their sides, each with a small arrow embedded in its throat.

Pieter's cries brought the rest to him within seconds despite the brandy they'd drunk earlier, for all were experienced in the bush and the ability to wake from sound slumber to instant alertness was part of the discipline for survival.

They stood silently looking down at their dead mounts, every man aware that without horses the return home would be difficult indeed. They had not brought pack animals, not planning to go so far, and wishing to travel light for the hunt.

They carried all their supplies with them and had enough for their week away, but no more.

'God rot those little yellow heathens,' Tiaan Koorts spat.

'Now they HAVE to be taken care of once and for all.' He had forgotten that identical words had passed his lips only half a day since.

'Ja,' nodded Styger, embarrassed that he'd fallen asleep on his watch, and relieved that Pieter had not mentioned it. 'At first light we go up, eh?'

Malan spat his agreement vehemently. He'd lost two horses in as many days and wanted satisfaction.

When Pieter reminded them of the wounded man, and offered to stay with him, his father rounded on him.

'Oh no, *meisie*, you don't get out of it that way. You're coming with us. The Englishman will be all right until we get back. The cowardly little *boggers* that did this will be hiding back in their holes by now.'

Of course he was as wrong in this as in so many things.

As the four white men set out on foot, just as the sun was appearing over the peaks of the Drakensberg, two pairs of eyes watched them disappear from view up the mountain. Then they moved silently into the camp.

Gian and Xinob had two reasons for not returning to the cave during the night.

The man lying by the fire had killed their friend Raan, and the rest of the whiteskins were heading away from the direction of the cave.

After a two hour walk straight up, the white men veered to the left and followed a valley, stopping at a small waterfall to rest and drink their fill.

Tiaan suddenly held up a hand for silence. He looked around and received a nod from Malan and a blank look from the German. His son looked down at his boots. He too had heard the sounds moving down through the bush, and his heart was heavy at what was to come.

The three women carried ostrich shells and clay pots for transporting water back to the home cave. In front and behind skipped the children, three girls and two boys.

The boys were tiny but well proportioned like their fathers, and each had a length of dead wood which they used as bows and they fired pretend arrows into imaginary animals as they passed.

The girls were of different ages and only the oldest had that accumulation of fat on her buttocks known as steatopygia, and which could be lived off when food was scarce. She also carried water vessels while the two younger girls played and chatted in the strange click sounds that was the language of the Bushmen.

As they approached the rocks at the foot of the waterfall, one of the women stopped and held her head back, elevating her nose as she sniffed the air. She lowered her head and looked around at the trees and bushes, surrounding the edge of the rock pool that had been formed by centuries of water falling from above.

The first bullet, fired by Tiaan Koorts, took the back of her head off and a mixture of shattered bone and brain fluid splashed over the two younger girls at her side. Shrill screams echoed around the pool as Malan and Styger both fired at the woman kneeling to fill a clay pot; one bullet catching her in the side and ripping through internal organs, and the other shattering an elbow and almost severing the lower arm.

One of the boys went down next, a small circle where his right eye had been and a large exit hole appearing in the back of his head. The older girl was bringing up the rear of the group, and had just reached the edge of the path when the firing began. She dropped her pots and ran. Styger had just put a bullet into the stomach of the third woman when he saw the girl disappear.

He was closest to the path and left his position to go after her.

In the meantime the remaining two riflemen continued firing down into the small amphitheatre. Tiaan Koorts was reminded of the expression much loved by the English of 'shooting fish in a barrel'. He had never quite understood it before, but now he did. The other boy began running straight to the group of rocks where Malan was concealed, and when he was less than two metres away the trader put a bullet between his eyes.

The small head exploded like an over-ripe melon and a great gout of blood and gore shot in every direction, some splashing over the rocks and covering the top part of the rifleman. His wide brimmed hat and beard dripped blood, giving him a frightening aspect.

Ten metres to his right, Tiaan Koorts rose to his feet, a look of wild triumph on his face. He looked down at the carnage below the waterfall and was silent for a few moments. Two of the women lay at the edge of the pool, and the third floated face down. The crimson waters lapped gently at her body.

The children were more spread out, the two girls having tried to escape the murderous rain of bullets by running towards the waterfall, only to find no way up the sheer wall.

There they died, each tiny body almost blown apart from the same heavy bullets that the white men would use to bring down the elephant and the rhino.

'Where the hell's that boy?' Tiaan roared suddenly, no longer interested in the results of the morning's work.

'Where's Willie, for that matter?' Malan shrugged as he climbed to his feet. 'He's probably gone after the other one, the girl. You know his eyes are blinkered when his blood heats up.'

'The devil curse the man,' Koorts growled. He prided himself on being a good churchman, and on Sundays he would drive his family to town early so he could assist the dominie with the service, and the thought of a white man lying with a heathen turned his stomach.

To shoot them was one thing, but that...

The subject of his anger had been fortunate, for at first the Bushman girl had eluded him with ease, fear lending speed to her flight as she heard the big whiteskin crashing behind her. But she made the mistake of turning to see if he gained, and stumbled over a tree root, crashing heavily off the path and rolling down a steep slope into a small clearing.

There was a loud crack as the fibula in her right leg broke cleanly above the ankle. The girl tried to regain her feet and cried aloud at the pain as her leg collapsed beneath her.

A shadow appeared above where she lay, and she looked up into the closely set eyes of the German. He was doing something with the front of his clothing, and although his words were meaningless to her, her eyes went wide in understanding.

He had bared himself completely and was reaching down to tear the scrap of *dassie* hide from her waist, still uttering his obscene intentions, when he felt the cold metal on his neck.

'I do not think you should be doing this, *Meneer* Styger,' the voice had a tremor in it and sweat ran down the face of its owner, for this was the first time Pieter Koorts had ever held a gun on a fellow human being.

'You young fool,' the German bent to pull up his trousers and the ring of metal was forced deeper into his skin until he stood quite still. 'Leave now and I will forget this, otherwise...'

'Otherwise nothing, *meneer*,' the young man was looking at the pitifully small figure on the ground. He did not see a misshapen creature from the Stone Age, with peppercorn hair and protruding backside, wearing a tiny piece of fur for clothing. He saw only a frightened girl child, with a broken piece of bone protruding from her damaged leg.

He also saw the hulking figure standing over her, his manhood exposed and his purpose clear, and Pieter Koorts felt sudden anger. An anger that had been building in him for a very long time.

Styger mistook the younger man's stillness for uncertainty, and when the pressure of the barrel left his neck he spun quickly to knock the rifle aside.

Only to find it was no longer there. Pieter held it across his body now and as the German moved menacingly towards him, he tripped over his pants and fell forward. Pieter lashed out with the barrel, catching Styger high on the face.

The foresight laid his forehead open to the bone and he gave a great bellow of pain. Blinded now because of the blood pouring down into his eyes, Styger's arms reached for the cause of his pain.

It seemed to Pieter that he had been taken from his body and elevated to some high place from where he gazed down on the scene below. Surely it was not he who slammed the stock of the rifle up hard between the German's legs, then waited for the man to topple forward to his knees before kicking him full in the face?

And was it the same young man who picked up the pathetically light form of the child and ran off into the bush? The same reader of poetry who stopped when he could go no further, and made a shelter beneath the branches of a fallen ironwood? He knew as he set her leg by pushing the broken ends together and used two straight sticks as splints, finally binding them in place with strips of shirt from his back, that it really was himself.

The girl had passed out as he began to force the bone fractures together, and now as he felt her eyes upon him he smiled gently at her. She no longer seemed frightened, as though she knew that he meant her no harm, and she touched her leg wonderingly and looked up at him. Her lips drew back from the strong teeth in a strange grimace that Pieter somehow knew was a smile.

The two remaining hunters left the waterfall with mixed feelings. They were satisfied they'd killed seven of the creatures they despised, yet felt something that was hard to put into words. If they had been capable of seeing themselves more honestly, they might have recognised it as shame.

Instead they intended to palliate their consciences by compounding their deeds. They decided to backtrack the water party to where they could locate the rest of the tribe and wipe them out once and for all.

At one point, as Koorts and Malan followed the trail upwards, they passed within metres of Willie Styger, lying unconscious below them. If they had been a few minutes earlier, Tiaan Koorts might possibly have glimpsed his son and heir running into the trees with a strange bundle in his arms.

But they did not, and so they continued on the narrow trail as it swept around to the left of the high feature, which they were soon to become an integral part of.

The German came out of his enforced slumber feeling like a *veldt* dog's supper. His testicles had swollen to twice their size and he could not touch them without feeling nauseous and blacking out again. The blood had stopped on his forehead and he could feel the embossed ridge running across below the hairline. He felt his nose gingerly and did not require a surgeon to confirm it was broken.

His eyes were beginning to close with sympathetic bruising from the nose, and he rejected his first reaction to go after the perpetrator of his pain and misery straight away.

Instead he pulled up his moleskin trousers, climbed painfully back to the path, then staggered down to the waterfall pool.

The German leaned against a tree and gazed down at the scene below, the small bodies sprawled in grotesque positions of death, unaware of what had struck them down so suddenly. He felt nothing but elation that he had been one of those unknown instruments of death, and that other feeling that had rested, albeit lightly, on his accomplices' shoulders, did not touch Styger in the slightest.

He moved down, and around to the far side of the pool, ignoring the smell and sight of death, and drank deeply of the falling waters. He plunged his face beneath the cascade and wiped it gently on his sleeves, then continued back to the previous night's camp.

There he would find food and ammunition, the medical supplies, and brandy. Especially the brandy.

Some attention to his wounds, a good hot meal, and a warm night's sleep helped along with several draughts of brandy, and he would be ready to go back up and sort out that young *bogger*, Pieter Koorts. And to hell with his old man if he wanted to get in the way.

It was an hour from last light when Willie Styger stumbled into the camp.

The Englishman still lay beside the fire, burning surprisingly well considering the time that had elapsed since they'd been gone.

Only as he drew closer did he see what made it burn so well.

The ground around the fire glittered white with sugar and salt, and the smell of burnt food pervaded the air.

His foot kicked against something and he glanced down to find a piece of saddle, and when he took a closer look around he saw that all of their gear and supplies were gone. It had been burned, for as he gazed closer at the edges of the fire he saw the remains of blankets and food.

Styger moved slowly to the lone form on the far side of the fire. Prentice-Smythe was lying on his side and the German grasped a shoulder and pulled him onto his back. He jumped as the empty eye sockets gazed blankly back, the lipless mouth grinning inanely.

With a stifled curse the big forester drew his sidearm and dropped slowly into a crouch, wincing at the pain between his legs. From that position he rotated slowly to peer carefully into the surrounding undergrowth, the hammer pulled back and his second joint taking first pressure on the trigger.

He looked everywhere but above, and the arrow struck downwards almost vertically, pinning his right arm into his right thigh as it rested there. He cursed with pain and tried to pull it out, only to have it fall to pieces when his hand grasped it. He threw down the thin haft of the arrow and grabbed for his pistol, peering blindly into the trees above him.

The second Bushman arrow struck him in the face as he looked up, finding its mark to the left of his nose and below the eye, and the poisoned tip penetrated the roof of his mouth and pinned tongue to lower jaw.

The gun dropped and he rolled slowly onto his back, gazing up at the darkening sky as he felt the poison begin its painful work.

Xinob was moving swiftly through the bush in a direct line for the home cave, when he heard the noise of the white man's thunder off to his right. He decided they had found a buck drinking at the pool beneath the falling water, and were indulging in the over-kill that was their way. The visibility of the day was fast disappearing as he arrived on the flat place outside the cave. It was nearly thirty minutes since he'd heard the last sound from the white man's guns, and he reasoned they would soon be back in their camp.

He was pleased as he thought of their dismay when they discovered the state of their camp, and their companion.

They could do nothing until morning, and by then Xinob would have the rest of the band many miles away, high up into the pass of the next valley. Gian would join them after a night spent harassing the Whites, and depriving them of the sleep they seemed to need so much.

He saw the cooking fire tended by an old woman, the mother of Raan, and his heart was heavy that he would have to tell her of her son's death. Several small children played at the cave mouth and he saw two older women preparing skins for the cold days ahead. His own wife, and the wives of Gian and Raan, were not in sight. Nor the older daughter of Raan, a beauty already who would soon to be ready to mate, and who had been promised to Oba. Two of his other children were missing also, and Xinob became worried.

He entered the cave and began speaking rapidly in that strange series of clicks and clucks that made a French missionary once likened their language to the sound of turkeys.

The replies he received threw him into consternation, for now he knew the meaning of the whiteskin's thunder, and was aware it had not been a buck at the water hole.

His first thought was to go swiftly to that place but then he realised his immediate responsibility lay with those who remained in the cave. The others must now be dead. Though he wept inside for his wife and his children, he did not let his emotions interfere with what had to be done, for he was *San*.

He told them quickly what must have happened to the water carriers, and made the women wrap the essential cooking equipment in hides for carrying. He replenished his arrows from the cache at the back of the cave, but otherwise carried nothing. He must be free to fight on their journey away from the Whites.

The children were aged between two years and seven, and there were five of them. The two younger women, one was Xinob's own mother, carried the two smallest children, although they were already heavily burdened. At last they lined up outside the cave, ready to run once more from their enemies. Xinob took the lead and had moved only a little way down the path when he was halted by the furious clicking from the old crone at the rear.

Although the day had gone now, the feeble rays of a pale and watery moon gave the whole area an eerie visibility. The two hunters had no difficulty in finding targets, and the first bullet took the top of the old one's head off. The shots continued to ring out and none could fail to find a target along the narrow trail. Xinob turned to face the enemy, an arrow already in his bow and straining for flight, but he could not get a clear shot at the whiteskins.

The mother of Raan was before him and her bare chest suddenly opened, bursting outwards like the petals of a flower that took but a second to bloom. He was covered in bone and flesh and innards, and a fine pink spray seemed to hang on the cold evening air.

He moved to one side and a bullet shattered his right shoulder, and he realised too late that the woman had been the only one left between himself and the whiteskins.

Behind her, sprawled in an untidy line along the path, lay the remains of his tribe.

His bow dropped from him as another piece of lead tore a kneecap away and knocked him to the ground. He was struggling to pull his stone knife when the last bullet ripped through his left pectoral and deep into his heart. Xinob did not feel it, for the spirit was already departing his body now his people were gone.

All except Gian the leader, who would avenge them before they met again in the spirit land. Xinob died at peace with this thought, and when the two Boers looked down at the little Bushman they were puzzled by the look on his face, yet perhaps they could be forgiven for not recognising it.

Given the circumstances, the last thing they would have expected was a look of triumph.

When Gian heard the first of the whiteskin thunder he concluded the same as Xinob, that they were blasting some lone buck at the water pool. When the big bearded one had walked into the camp alone he had thought him the lead man, and he could not ignore that chance. After the kill he had descended the tree and dragged the heavy body into the bush.

He had then waited for the rest to appear and prepared himself for the long night ahead. He found a depression behind a fallen log, where he feasted off fat grubs and lay down to rest.

The Bushman does not need much sleep, and a few minutes nap could refresh him for a long time, but the day had been long. So it was dark when he awoke, and at first he thought it had been the return of the white men that had awakened him.

Then he heard the noise far off, the sounds of the sticks that spat death.. Only then did he remember the earlier sounds and wonder at them, before finally arriving at the same conclusion as Xinob.

The fire had died out now as the little Bushman circled the camp and began to run towards the place where the water came down from above. His pace was swift, for his eyes could see as clearly as by day and he knew he would hear the whiteskins long before they would be aware of him.

The Bushman holds anguish and pain close to his heart. He does not shed tears as does the white man, but who is to say he does not feel it to any lesser degree. Strong men weep inside, but they weep nonetheless.

When Gian gazed down upon the place where the water falls he wore no expression and his face was dry, but half of his people were down there and none would sing or dance around the fire again. His wife lay there and two of his children. The oldest was dead, buried on the *veldt* a day away, and the youngest would be at the home cave.

He did not go down to the pool and he did not try to bury his dead. That was for later, after he had avenged them. For how else could their shades sleep in peace beneath the same land that had seen their death, knowing their murderers still breathed?

The little Bushgirl moaned softly in her sleep and Pieter Koorts felt helpless. He knew she was in pain but there was nothing he could do for her and he consoled himself with the knowledge she was at least alive.

They both heard the shooting and the girl had seen the pain in his eyes, and wondered at the strange white man. She too had an awareness of what was happening to the remainder of her people.

But she also possessed the eternal fatalism of the San, and made no outward show of her pain.

He'd had *biltong* and hardtack biscuits in his pockets and shared these with the little creature he found himself responsible for. A determination had grown inside the young man, and a hardness and awareness of himself had grown with it. He had done nothing to stop what had gone before, and deep inside he knew there was little he could have done to prevent it, but she would live and he swore this before his God.

She had taken the sustenance timidly, and ate it slowly. By now she realised the tall whiteskin with the golden hair meant her no harm. She tried to repay him in kind, by crawling to a rotting log and digging out fat juicy worms, but he declined with a smile.

Pieter had thrown his coat over the small figure and now he sat with his back resting against the fallen tree, thinking of what he should do in the morning. If his father and his friends had indeed wiped out the rest of the Bushmen, where could the girl go? Like any creature of the wild she would not survive in civilisation, even if he could succeed in getting her down to the *veldt* and to the farm.

In any case, when his father returned he would show no mercy in finishing his self appointed task. His troubled thoughts gave way to troubled dreams as Pieter fell into a fitful doze, from which he was awakened by frantic clicking from the injured girl.

His eyes opened to see a dark figure outlined against the night sky, and moonlight reflected two glints of light from eyes that appeared almost feral.

Pieter knew he faced death by a Bushman arrow, for he could see the shape of the drawing arm projecting to the side, but he did not move to defend himself nor cry out in mitigation, for he knew neither could succeed.

The bowman would have two arrows in him before he could reach his pistol, and also they did not share a language. He was also patently aware of the great crimes committed on this man's people.

By HIS people, and he resigned himself for whatever was to come. The clicking stopped and the Bushman replied rapidly in kind, followed by a silence. Still the young white man did not move or speak, and to his surprise found he was unafraid. He did not know why this should be.

The shadow moved over to the girl and the clicks became softer, and they spoke at length before the little man rose to his feet and approached Pieter. He did not know what to expect but remained still for he could see his death now as an honourable thing, whereas his former companions would rot for eternity.

But death was not seeking Pieter Koorts that night, nor would it for many nights to come, but that is not part of our story and belongs to a much longer one.

A small hand touched his shoulder briefly, then the Bushman was gone.

Tiaan Koorts and Johann Malan finished their task of pushing the bodies over the edge of the path. They stoked up the remains of the cooking fire and ate what biltong and stale biscuits they had left. Food was secondary to the half bottle of brandy that remained.

They talked long into the night these men of the *veldt*, each a fervent worshipper in his own way. One from High Dutch descent, and the other enjoying that freedom of worship that his persecuted Huguenot forebears had never known. Both were married and had children, and for the most part were good husbands and fathers. They were hard working, and drank lustily yet without causing distress to their families or their fellows.

They would no more think of stealing or cheating than they would of killing someone or stealing away his wife. For the laws of God were the laws they lived by. Men like Koorts and Malan received their instructions from the first half of an old book, which was either the word of God or the earliest recorded history of man.

This depended on your belief.

The content of that book was open to wide interpretation, and could provide justification for an act, as easily as it could show damnation for that deed, and they had long discussed the former.

The two men sat and drank and smoked their pipes; sheltered now in the same cave which had housed the men, women and children they had murdered in cold blood.

They felt neither remorse nor sorrow, and they would have been indignant if the word guilt had been mentioned in their presence.

They had come to hunt, and they had not been disappointed.

They did not regard what they had done as the genocide of a small tribe, but the extermination of a pack of vermin. They had performed a service to their people and now their cattle would be safe.

A century later other farmers in the Drakensberg would use a similar excuse to try and kill the last of a species, this time the magnificent *lammergeier,* whom they said killed the young lambs. They ignored the fact, or chose not to see it, that the *lammergeier* was a carrion eater and never killed to eat.

So they sat, content for the moment though still aware they would face problems when the sun came up. One of their number was dead, two lost, and another injured. They also had no horses. But it would come right, they assured each other. Once they'd joined the rest and made a litter for the Englishman.

'Unless he's already dead,' Malan said with a hopeful wink, and Tiaan Koorts laughed loudly as he reached for the bottle.

He froze as he looked across the fire into the dark, and his eyes locked on the same animal-like ones as had his son a few hours earlier. Gian had slipped off the path and come upon the cave from the bush below. Where he had found the rest of his people.

His bow was drawn yet he did not release the string. He wanted to examine these killers of women and children with his own eyes, as though by looking hard enough he might see what made them as they were. He knew all Whites were not bad to the Bushmen, just as all Blacks were not, for his grandfather had told of when the black men and the San had inhabited these valleys alongside one another for many generations.

The one with the head of gold had saved Nia's life by fighting another White, and then tending her wound, but these who sat before him were less than the cowardly *hyaena* who came only against the weak and the...

He saw a whiteskin dive away from the fire and grab for his long thunder stick, and Gian moved the bow a few inches and sent his arrow into the man's neck. His hand was a blur as another arrow was taken from his side quiver, nocked, drawn, and released in the space it takes a man to blink an eyelid.

It flew across the cave and struck the rear wall, for as soon as Malan had moved so too did Koorts, and he already had his pistol drawn and firing before his friend's body had struck the floor.

The little Bushman felt fire enter his side and run through him. Another pain went into his left hand and he could no longer grasp the wood of his bow as it fell at his feet.

The white man was standing now, his small thunderstick pointing at Gian's head. The little Bushman looked up into the eyes of the giant and knew there was no mercy there. Nor did he expect any.

His glanced away from the tall figure of Tiaan Koorts to the wall behind, his eyes half closed and his lips moved slowly, and the sounds that came from them were low and soft.

'Praying will do you no good, heathen,' the farmer said, not unkindly. 'It is not for the likes of you, for God hears only...'

There was a sound behind him and Koorts turned quickly, his finger curling on the trigger...

Two hours before the dawn spread fingers of light over the mountains and valleys, Pieter Koorts picked up the feather light form of the Bushgirl. In his world she was ugly, being small and stunted, with strange clumps on her head instead of hair, and her backside was huge and ungainly to his western eyes.

But to the young Boer she was simply a wounded denizen of the bush. He saw her not as a human or a non-human, neither an animal nor less than one, but another warm blooded creature needing help.

He climbed back to the narrow bush trail and followed it upward with difficulty. Whenever he hesitated, casting his eyes around for the path, a tiny hand would point unerringly and he would pick it up once more.

Finally they arrived near the big cave and Pieter could see the glow of a fire. He placed his little bundle down carefully and went forward quietly, drawn pistol in hand, and fearful now for what he might find.

The first thing he saw was the blazing fire and this spoilt his vision for a few minutes until he covered his eyes and put his back to it. Then he saw the body of Johann Malan lying against a rock with the butt of his rifle poking out from under his body. Pieter saw the arrow protruding from his neck.

He heard a grunt and saw a Bushman propped against a dead tree on the far side of the entrance, and somehow knew this was their nocturnal visitor. He knelt by the helpless little figure and found the deep furrow in his side where the bullet had ploughed through.

Pieter took off his neckerchief and soaked it in the large pot by the mouth of the cave, then cleaned the wound as best he could. As he looked up he found the Bushman's eyes upon him. He smiled gently and the little face appeared to try to imitate him.

He reached for his hand, then saw the blood where the bullet had gone through. He tore the cloth in two and wrapped half around the wounded hand, using the other half on his side. He then carried him over to the fire and propped him against a log which had obviously been used for seating.

Pieter then went and carried the girl back, placing her close to the fire next to the man. He found clay bowls and gave them both water, then warmed himself by the fire and listened to their chatter for a while. Eventually he wandered off to look around the cave in search of food and skins to sleep on.

It was then he found his father.

The body was lying behind a large rock in the rear of the cave, and he fetched a burning branch from the fire. By its light he could see the crumbled figure, wedged half against the wall of the cave and the rock, and he recognised his clothing; the thick moleskin pants and the woven Boer coat. With difficulty Pieter managed to drag his father into the open and roll him over.

The sight made him turn away in horror and it was a little while before he could force himself to look at it again. He was torn almost beyond recognition, and only when he held the torch down lower did he see the lacerations were in regular lines.

Like the claws of a big cat.

The same track-like wounds were right down his front, clothing and flesh joined together as they hung like strips of drying *biltong* from his chest and stomach. The face was the worst, great gouges revealed the gleaming white of the skull beneath, and both eyes had been sliced through and lay half out of their sockets. The strong full nose he had seen across the dining table all the days of his life, was divided, and the flesh flopped down on either side.

The same razor edge that caused such a dreadful wound had continued down to mutilate the lips and chin, during which the tongue had been caught and ripped almost out, hanging now on one thin strip of white sinew.

Pieter Koorts rolled the body of his father onto its front again and went over to the water pot, where he threw handfuls of water over his face, as though purging his eyes from what they had seen.

Both of the injured San looked up at him. He saw sorrow in the girl's eyes but something quite different in the man's. It was not triumph, as Xinob had shown to the whiteskins who had killed him, but a look that in later years Pieter would describe as profundity, a look of knowledge and wisdom beyond all the attainments of the white race.

He sat by the fire with his back resting against the same log as the two Bushmen, and he was still there as dawn threw out her meagre offering of light.

Gian and the girl exchanged clicks, then the little man rose and walked down into the forest, while the girl dragged herself to the water container. There she filled a clay pot and placed it on the side of the fire to heat.

When Gian returned he carried an armful of roots and plants, which he handed to Nia. She prepared them and placed them in the pot, letting them simmer for a while, then added some red clay from the side of the cave. The resultant mixture was then spread on both their injuries, each taking it in turn to apply the poultice to the other.

It was past noon when Pieter came out of his self induced trance, and looked around in a dazed fashion.

The girl still lay by the fire, which had been made up with fresh wood, but there was no sign of the little Bushman. Peter gave the girl a soft smile and stood up. There was much to be done before he began the long journey back to the farm. His father and Johann Malan would have to be buried, and he suspected he would find two more bodies at the camp. He knew Bushmen buried their dead too, and he would help them.

He was thinking about hunting some game for them to eat when Gian appeared from the bush with the body of a grey *duiker* over his shoulder. His wounds no longer seemed to trouble him, and the poultice was still in place on his side. The hand was wrapped with Pieter's neckerchief over more of the healing mixture.

He threw his prize down in front of the girl, and an understanding passed between them. He was a good hunter and would be able to provide, despite his wounds and the threat of the white man. The little maid began to prepare the animal for cooking, and Pieter moved back into the cave and dragged out the two bodies. He used a flat piece of stone to scrape out a single shallow grave.

After placing the corpse of his father alongside that of the trader, he scraped the earth back over them and piled rocks on top. He finished his unpleasant but necessary task and returned to the cave.

The rich aroma of roasting venison assailed his nostrils as he drew near, and he was suddenly conscious of a powerful hunger. The Bushman sliced off a generous portion and handed it to the tall white man, the fatty juices running down his hands and arms. Pieter took it, tearing the meat greedily and swallowing quickly.

'Good,' he mumbled through another mouthful. 'It's very good.' The two bush people looked up from their own noisy feasting and the man showed his white teeth.

'Goo,' he slurred. 'T'ver goo.'

The young Afrikaaner stared for a moment, startled at the English words the Bushman had mimicked, and he knew beyond doubt that he was sitting and eating with intelligent people, despite their appearance and way of life.

He thought of the many clever people who had seen them as stunted creatures who spoke with the language of turkeys, and had never seen them for what they really were. A proud and intelligent race, who so chose to live in a peaceful and simple way, to hunt and live as their forebears had.

He began to laugh with cynical humour at the irony of it all, and the two little San, who would move higher into the mountains and produce two more generations before their tribe was gone for ever, joined in.

The hills rang with the strange sounds made by the ill-assorted trio, and the birds of the Drakensberg accompanied them; the Hoopoe and the fork-tailed Drongo, the Cape Wagtail and the Sandpiper, the Crowned Plover and the foolish Hadeda, and it seemed all of nature was relieved there was peace once more.

No matter how short a period it might last.

Pieter Koorts stood at the grave of his father. He was going home and his Bushman friend would guide him for part of the way. Gian's new wife, Nia, would pack for their move on his return.

In the past week they had become friends and learned to communicate with words from their own languages and in sign. Pieter's hope was that he would see them again, and this would be realised, for one day he would be an authority on the Bushman of the Drakensberg, and this was as it should be.

For he had known the last of them.

'You never understood, *vader*,' he said sadly, though he shed no tears for the man who lay beneath his feet. 'And you did not try to. That is your crime, as it is the crime, and the tragedy, of your generation. But I think you did at the end. Of this I am sure.'

And he clasped his hands in front of him and recited softly from the book his father had burned.

'That God, which ever lives and loves,

One God, one law, one element,

And one far-off divine event,

To which the whole creation moves.'

He thought again of his father's death, ripped to pieces by the claws of some huge cat, yet not the leopard or the cheetah who hunted these mountains. The spread of claws was too wide, the gouges too deep. Only a lion, and a big one, could have done such damage. Yet it was not their habitat, and there were no lions in the mountains.

Except for one. Painted on the wall of the Bushman cave.

Pieter picked up his rifle and turned away. Gian was waiting for him down the path. The Boer looked at the Stone Age man and wondered if he really had the power to bring a cave-drawing to life.

For when had Pieter touched the lion painting, the claws had been wet with blood.

CHAPTER TEN

Although he was awake before dawn the next day, the old man was already up. The fire had been cajoled back to life and the pot of water was bubbling away merrily.

The boy smiled as he gazed around the makeshift campsite, just one of many on their journey to the tall mountains. He would miss it all when they reached their destination, and his eventual return to Durban and his family, for he knew that must be. Some day soon.

In the meantime he would make the most of their time together. Just himself and the old man, alone in Africa, on a journey to the past. Or so it appeared to the romantic in him.

He quickly disentangled himself from his sleeping bag, not wishing to waste any of the new day, then stared in astonishment at Joseph. He had removed all of his clothing and was splashing water over himself from the tiny stream that trickled past.

'I am cleansing away the years of living among Whites,' he said without emotion. 'When I reach my homeland it will be as Kqwedi the warrior. Joseph the servant lives no more.'

He dried himself off on his shirt, which he tossed on the pile with his suit and shoes. From his leather bag he produced the trappings of an Amangwane warrior. They were similar to those of a Zulu - furs, skins, a head-dress and anklets. He donned them slowly, taking care with each piece and handling them almost reverently. The boy watched with a feeling of awe.

Finally he took out the main accoutrements of his standing in the world of the Ngwane. The cowhide shield and his fighting sticks. His bow went over his shoulders and an old quiver, made in the Bushman style from the bark of the *kokerboom* - quiver tree - was strapped to his side.

'You look terrific,' Michael breathed at last, and he was right. For the old man looked like the warrior he had been, so long ago.

'I must give praise to the Gods,' he said proudly. 'Today I fast, so eat and prepare to leave when I get back.'

The boy watched him stride purposefully through the bush, shoulders pulled back and head held high. He looked every inch the warrior, and it was as if the years had dropped from him.

Michael made himself tea and ate the remains of the birds. The *dassie* he would keep for lunch.

When he'd finished, he packed his things away and extinguished the fire, piling soil on top to prevent sparks escaping. He stood gazing thoughtfully at the spot his companion had disappeared, then began taking his own clothes off.

When the old man returned, it was his turn to look surprised. The boy was wearing the remains of his khaki shirt, torn into a strip and tied around his waist as a loincloth.

One of the sleeves was tied around his head, and the other his left ankle. He held two stout sticks which he'd cut from a thorn bush.

Joseph, known once more by his tribal name of Kqwedi, did not know whether to laugh or be honoured by the boy's comical attempt to emulate him. Wisely, he chose the latter.

When they set off, Michael wore his boots at the old man's insistence, but left his clothing piled near the rest.

'For whoever finds it,' he said carelessly, then added ominously. 'I have no further use for it.'

The warrior kept a straight face as he headed for the high peaks in the distance. They represented his waking thoughts over the many long years since he'd left them, and his dreams at night.

The Barrier of Uplifted Spears, his *uKhahlamba*.

The boy too looked on the far mountains with anticipation, for they were the accumulation of his own thoughts and dreams. Though not as old, they were every bit as real to him, and to breathe the air of the Berg alone would fulfil his life at that moment in time.

It was the last night before they reached the foothills of the Drakensberg. Then they would move northwards, following the line of the mountains to Cathedral Peak. There they would find the valleys of the Mnweni, and the Amangwane lands.

The warrior Kqwedi, once called Joseph, had used his bow to good effect in the late afternoon, and they had dined well on the grey *duiker* he had shot.

The elusive little buck feeds at night, the old man told the boy, and rests up during the day. He had found its tracks leading into a thick patch of scrub and thorn, and while Michael made a noise on the far side, he had waited with bow ready. It darted out zigzagging, then changed to long plunging jumps, but he was aware of its tricks and his first arrow sank into its neck.

While they ate, the rest of the meat slowly cooking for later consumption, the white boy felt he had never eaten tastier meat, and he pushed his usual qualms of conscience out of his mind. He admitted they were getting smaller each day.

He was looking at the old man expectantly, and a grizzled eyebrow was raised in return.

'What story are you going to tell tonight, Jo...Kqwedi?'

'Surely you are becoming too old for bedtime stories, Michael?' the old man teased. 'You wear the garb of a warrior now.'

This was partially true, for the old man had fashioned a proper head-dress and armbands from the *dassie* skin, and was already working on the *duiker* pelt to make a loincloth for him.

'I'll never be too old for one of your stories,' the boy replied stoutly.

'Alright,' the grey warrior chuckled. 'You have won me over, *jong*. But it will be your turn to tell one next.'

The boy nodded eagerly, and sat forward to catch the heat from the fire. The shadows were lengthening now, casting strange shapes on the boles of trees and showing sinister forms in the bush. Clouds rolled across the moon and the night was eerily still. The boy shivered again, and not from the cold alone.

As Michael had now discovered, the old man's command of English was good, and he was able to assume a different voice. It became lower as he began to speak, and its tone was enough to chill the blood of the young listener.

'About thirty years ago I worked in the diamond fields on the west coast of Namibia. Many tales are told of the precious stones, and many people worship them, none more than the white man. They represent power, and that alone is a fascination for certain kinds of men. This is a story I once heard, told by a White, and he swore it was true and he had read it in a newspaper.'

He paused to take out his battered pipe, and let the atmosphere soak into the receptive mind of his listener. Michael sat staring into the flames, already feeling that delicious thrill that is the prelude to fear itself. 'Who would have a motive to kill your wife, *meneer?*'

THE JAKKALSBERGE

The stocky man raised his head slowly. 'What does that mean? She was killed by burglars, wasn't she?'

'Perhaps, *Meneer*, perhaps,' the policeman murmured.

He was very large. This combined with his heavy Afrikaans accent gave the impression of a lumbering prop forward. He HAD in fact played prop forward for the Province in his younger days, and his usual gait could indeed be described as lumbering. But there the assumption, that brain and brawn do not go together, ended.

He took a plastic bag from a uniformed constable. 'Have you seen this before, *Mnr* Grobelaar?'

Paul Grobelaar stood up and moved over to the man in the crumpled shirt and trousers. He peered hard at the bag but made no attempt to touch it.

'Yes, it's my pistol,' he said finally, a note of self-criticism in his voice. 'They must have found it when they broke in. I keep it in the drawer by the bed, in case of a break-in during the night.'

Detective Warrant Officer van Zyl handed the murder weapon back to the constable, as the other man returned to his seat. He sank his head in his hands and muttered something in a low voice.

'I beg your pardon, *Meneer*?' the policeman queried.

'The diamond, man,' Grobelaar said loudly. 'It was the bloody diamond that killed her. They were right. it IS cursed.'

'You mean the Jakkalsberge, *Meneer*?'

'*Ja*, of course I mean the Jakkalsberge,' the businessman rose and poured himself neat whisky from the well-stocked bar. He proffered the bottle to the warrant officer.

'*Nee, Meneer, dankie*,' the shaggy head shook slightly. 'Was it taken? The diamond?'

'No. I destroyed it when...I found Tienie.' He gulped his whisky, replenishing it before he sat down again.

The big detective slumped into the chair opposite. 'I think you must tell me about it, *Meneer*,' he said in a not unkind voice.

The older man sipped slowly this time, his disturbed thoughts going back to the day he'd acquired the huge chunk of carbon crystal. Was it only three months since he'd first seen the Jakkalsberge?

The Jackal Mountains were in Namibia, once known as German South West Africa, and the Orange River ran past their southern end. In 1866 the daughter of a poor farmer had picked up the 21 carat Eureka from the Orange near the Hopetown district of the Cape Colony. In 1869 a Griqua shepherd boy found one of 83.5 carats, which he sold for 500 sheep, 10 oxen, and a horse. Surprisingly, not a lot of interest was shown at either of these incredible finds.

Finally, in 1870, a rich find at Klip Drift on the banks of the Vaal firmly established South Africa as a land rich in diamonds. Finds such as the pear-shaped Cullinan I, at 530 carats, and Cullinan II at 317 carats, caused many men to seek their fortunes in the tip of Southern Africa.

As Paul Grobelaar began to talk the detective sat quite still without interrupting, using his skills as an interrogative listener to good effect.

When the businessman had married Tienie Malan the previous year it had not changed him much on the surface. He was still the hard-nosed tycoon, where his ruthless acquisitions of companies were equalled only by the savage way he dissected and disposed of them for maximum profit.

His intense love for his wife, and his generosity toward her, were out-of-character traits that he kept to himself. These were all that he kept to himself, for his cruel methods were public knowledge in the business community. At 58 he was one of the wealthiest men in the Republic, which was something in a land that produced the Oppenheimers, the Ruperts and the Hertzogs. With the advent of Tienie he began to spend some of his wealth. There had been other women in his life, and he had given them gifts, but these had been purely business transactions.

Tienie was the first woman that he'd ever wanted to marry, and the wedding had been lavish, even by Capetonian standards. There had been many gifts during their first year together; clothes, jewellery, even an imported sports car. Tienie was thirty-two years his junior, and was always delighted with the presents he would fasten around her slender neck, attach to her tiny wrist, or slip on a delicate finger. None, of course, had been of such value as the Jakkalsberge Stone, yet it had come to him quite easily.

Without even costing a rand, in the literal sense.

Some time before he had begun to negotiate for a block of companies belonging to Kobus du Plessis from the Northern Cape. He was a man well into his seventies, a lay *dominie* in the Dutch Reform Church, who had retired many years before.

Due to the untimely death of his only son, he had been forced to resume the running of the small empire, though without the heart he once had. Before he was even aware of it, the shares in his businesses had changed hands, and one day he found they had all been bought up by Paul Grobelaar. Not that he cared much for any of them, anymore.

Except for the single company he had started with nearly fifty years before.

Knowing what would happen to it once Grobelaar got his *slagmes* - butcher's knife - into it, the old man took the unprecedented step of bearding the lion in his den. Sitting across the immense mahogany desk he found himself pleading for the return of his own first venture, and to a man who was every bit as unyielding as he had been warned. His eyes were hard as twin agates, and if anything could be read in his face it was a spiteful and pitiless humour, and not the understanding du Plessis sought.

'I want to keep it for my grandson, *Meneer*, for he is still young and it would be good to know that the business I started so long ago will still be in my family when I have made my peace with the Lord.'

'I bought and sold my first company within two months,' the stocky man replied. 'It took only that to carve it up into tiny pieces and sell it off to the carrion who waited. That's how I made my first million rand, and the way I've done it ever since.'

The old man rose, pride more than age causing the stiffness in his movements. 'I'll bid you *goeie more, Meneer*,' he said.

He picked up his hat and made for the door, but before he reached it the third person in the room spoke for the first time.

Richard Appleby had been Paul Grobelaar's assistant and confidante for over twelve years. His official job description was private secretary, and he knew everything there was to know about his employer and his business methods. As well as his private passions.

'Mr Grobelaar believes that you still have in your possession the diamond known as the Jakkalsberge, Mr du Plessis,' he said politely. 'In which case it might be possible that an agreement could be reached about the future of Du Plessis Engineering.'

The old man released his grip on the door handle and turned slowly back into the room. 'The diamond?'

'The diamond, Mr du Plessis,' the English accent was authentic, for Appleby was not South African born. 'I understand it is a blue white, colourless, and it weighs about 76 carats. If you wish to retain your company, clear and unencumbered of mortgages, bonds or shares, then an exchange could be effected.'

Du Plessis was old, but he was not frail, and yet he seemed now to have difficulty in moving his limbs as he tottered back to the huge desk. He sat down slowly and closed his eyes as though in pain.

'You must understand, contrary to what you are thinking, that there is nothing I would rather do than give you that accursed stone, *Mnr* Grobelaar,' he said slowly. 'But it is something my conscience will not easily let me do, much as I despise you.'

The man behind the desk smiled coldly, but it was again the Englishman who spoke. 'We know the stone is reputedly cursed, but so is the Hope, without much evidence to support that reputation.'

The old man spoke in a voice so low that the listeners had to lean forward to catch his words. 'It is not called the Jakkalsberge because it was found there, *Meneers*. Its first owner was a prospector named McBain, and he found it on the banks of the Oranje to the north of Prieska. That was in 1869, and the place would later become major diamond diggings.

'McBain had two partners but he never told them of his find, and late one night he slipped away and followed the Orange River in the direction of the sea. Perhaps he intended to find a ship at Orangemund, but he never made it. His partners were suspicious at his sudden departure and followed him. They caught up with him at the Jackal mountains, where they killed him and took the diamond.'

'And that's why they say it's cursed, eh?' Grobelaar laughed derisively.

The old man looked at him and shook his head. 'That was only the beginning. One of the partners, Greeley, killed the other, and was later caught and hanged. The diamond passed into the hands of the government, where it was sold at auction and went to America. There it was not heard of through several generations before it appeared again in Paris in 1932 and found its way back to Africa. Those several generations suffered the curse of the stone, *meneers*.

Every person who touched it found only misfortune, and although not all of them died themselves, someone near to them always did. Always.'

'You son died in a car accident, Mr du Plessis,' Appleby reminded him. 'There was nothing mysterious about his death and neither, I would think, was there in any of the others. Perhaps coincidence is the great leveller here?'

The old man was about to cite recent examples of the stone's infamy, when Grobelaar chose that moment to interrupt.

'You're talking *kak*, man,' he said rudely. 'If you believe that rubbish then you should jump at the chance to get rid of it, you old fraud. You're trying to talk me out of it, or raise the price. Either way don't bulldust me, *dominie*.'

Perhaps it was the insulting way he accented the title of which the old man was so proud, or it may have been the accusation of lying. Whichever it was, it worked.

'It is yours, *Meneer,*' he said with a decisiveness that should have been a warning to the two men. 'You want the Jakkalsberge, then you shall have it.'

'There will obviously be a cash difference,' Appleby said smoothly. 'Which Mr Grobelaar will be pleased to make up. Within reason, of course.'

'Not necessary,' the old man's voice had taken on a firmness it lacked when he'd entered the room. 'I will take no money for the stone, and make no profit from it. I want only what is rightfully mine; clear and unencumbered as you have said. Much pleasure may it give you, *Mnr* Grobelaar.'

The pleasure it gave Paul Grobelaar in bestowing it was more than equalled by the pleasure its possession gave his young bride, and her gratitude was amply shown in the nights ahead.

Three months later she was dead, and now her grieving husband finished his story to the patient detective.

'So tonight you arrived home and discovered the body of your wife, *Meneer?*' the large man asked in his deep voice, but as the question was rhetorical he continued without waiting for confirmation. 'Why did they not find the diamond? And how, and why, did you destroy it?'

The man opposite raised his head. 'It was well hidden, very well hidden. I smashed it into tiny pieces with a hammer, in the dining room hearth. As for why, surely that's obvious after what I...'

The policeman rose to his impressive height and looked down at the smaller man. There was even a note of apology in his voice, though it was belied by the contents of his words.

'I'm placing you under arrest for the murder of your wife, *Meneer.* Anything you say may...'

'What the hell are you talking about, man?' the businessman stood up angrily. 'What motive could I have for killing my wife. I loved her dearly, and why would I destroy a diamond worth millions if it wasn't all true?'

'Jealousy has always been a strong motive, *Meneer*,' the detective told him. 'Your wife had been having an affair for some time. When you found out about it, I can understand your disappointment and anger.'

'You're crazy, man,' Grobelaar had gone pale beneath his tan. 'I don't believe that, you're making it up, you *bogger*. It MUST have been burglars. I was at a meeting all evening with my assistant. Speak to him, he'll confirm it.'

'We already have, *meneer*,' the policeman said slowly, as though making certain that his words sank in. '*Mnr* Appleby denies seeing you at all tonight, but he does admit the affair with your wife.'

He laid a gentle hand on the other man's arm and led him into the dining room. 'If it was indeed burglars, as you say, why did they not take that?'

Paul Grobelaar stared down at the magnificent diamond lying on the dining table, light from the wall sconces scintillating from the perfectly cut facets.

The same diamond that he had smashed to pieces only an hour before. The stone with the curse he hadn't believed in.

The Jakkalsberge.

CHAPTER ELEVEN

'Wow,' Michael shook his head. 'And the man who told that story claimed it was true?'

The old head nodded gravely, though there was a twinkle in his eye that the boy did not see. Some magic he believed in. The magic of the earth, and the sky. Even some of the magic of his people, the healing magic, and the evil magic that causes men to destroy themselves. But the magic told by a white man, well, he wasn't too sure of that.

'Do you have a tale ready, Michael,' Joseph asked. 'A small one perhaps, or it can wait for the end of another day, for I am tired and must get my rest. Tomorrow will be filled with great excitement for me.'

The boy thought for a moment then looked up with a big grin. 'Yes, I have another story about my grandfather, and it won't take long at all.'

THE CURE

When my mother was ten years old her father sold his sugar farm in the Transvaal and bought a farm to the north west of Bloemfontein in the *Oranje Vrystaat* - the Orange Free State, near where he'd been born.

Between the Orange River and its principal tributary, the Vaal, lies a rolling prairie about 1400 metres above sea level. It floods with sunshine; green and warm in summer, and brown and crisply cold in winter. From one horizon to another this prairie-land stretches away, with the winds like a whispering siren's voice tempting the traveller ever onwards, with only a distant hillock to act as beacon on a journey seemingly without end.

The soil is deep and rich, and the surface only gently undulating, with nearly 30,000 farms covering these central plains. The area has always been regarded as one of the principal pantries of the continent of Africa, and my grandfather's farm lay in the portion drained by the Vaal River, where he grew huge fields of wheat, maize, sorghum, groundnuts, sunflowers, oats, potatoes, onions, barley, peas, beans, lucerne and buckwheat. The towns were small inhabited islands scattered at random in this ocean of cultivation.

In former years the Bushmen hunted the plains game; *springbok, blesbok, hartebeest, gnu and qwagga*, which lived there in herds so large their numbers were beyond count. The sound of the guns of the European hunters was an incessant voice of doom, until the game animals were almost completely eliminated. Sadly, the *gnu* and *qwagga* are now gone forever.

But as a girl of ten my mother knew little of these things, and would have cared less if they'd been told to her. She was happy to explore the fields and the workers *kraals*. These were Suthu, or Basotho as they call themselves, who came from Lesotho. They were a happy go lucky people, but not the hardest working race on earth, as my grandfather would often exclaim with a laugh.

Not that he openly mocked, or was ever cruel to his workers.

On the contrary, as I mentioned before, he was considered quite soft by the standards of his fellow-farmers. Despite my mother's tender and uninformed years, she knew he was an unusually kind and caring man at a time when such attitudes were not considered proper for a White to have for his Blacks. Especially a Boer farmer.

He paid them well, and each week with their wages they would receive a portion of meat, flour and sugar. Blankets and cooking utensils would be given to them on a regular basis.

My grandfather's hobby, for want of a better word, was doctoring.

At every opportunity he would reach for the battered medical bag that he'd found years ago, and from it he would produce all manner of medicines, potions and other cures, to the distraction of his *indunas*.

All was quite well, however, until the return of Sammy Sukubu. Now Sammy was a young man who had been rather bright at the local Mission school, and had been sent away to Bloemfontein to improve his education. He'd been taught to read and write in English and Afrikaans, but had shown no real aptitude for any other subjects. He had worked as a porter in the local hospital there.

Not long after his return to the workers *kraal* things began to go wrong on the farm. The work was not done to the usual standard, and items went missing. Many of the Suthus were loyal to my grandfather and one of the *indunas*, or sub-chiefs, told him what was occurring.

'Ah,' said my uncle wisely. 'So young Sammy is becoming a bush lawyer, is he?'

But instead of sorting the problem out there and then, my uncle left it with a chuckle and Sammy went on to greater strengths. During his stay in Bloemfontein he'd joined the local chapter of a political group, whose roots were firmly entwined with Moscow. Returning to the farm his mandate was to provoke as much trouble as he could.

It was here that his hospital experience held him in good stead. He had come back bearing a stout little book covered in blue cloth, and containing the symptoms of more than two hundred diseases and ailments of the body.

Simon Sekubu was the first to complain of severe abdominal pains. *Sekubu* means 'place of the hippopotamus' in Suthu, and referred to the place he was born. Simon - my uncle was a devout follower of the Dutch High Church, and had given all his workers Biblical names - was a good worker but easily led. He now manifested all the correct symptoms for constipation.

'It is bad, *baas*?' Simon managed to get out, bravely gritting his teeth. 'Will I not be able to work today?'

'No work for you today, Simon,' my uncle shook his head gravely. 'Not for the rest of the week, either.'

As he left the *rondavel* he heard Simon croak his thanks, though it sounded more like a suppressed chuckle. He said nothing.

That night after dinner my grandfather took over the kitchen, much to my grandmother's consternation. She had just finished clearing away the plates and cooking utensils when he walked in and began pulling bottles out of cupboards and mixing things in bowls.

Soon a strange, vile smell pervaded the house. It was unlike anything I had ever smelled before. It was reminiscent of some creature long dead, like a *kudu* I'd found in a cave once and I was sick to my stomach. But the stench of that dead antelope was nothing to the foul brew my uncle was concocting. He disappeared outside into the darkness, and returned with handfuls of herbs and plants, which he cheerfully crunched up into the big black pot on the hob.

When my grandmother hurried my mother off to bed, he was still at it, whistling tunelessly to himself as he stirred the awful stuff.

My mother made sure she was up early the next morning, though in truth she could not have lain in bed any longer. The aroma of the night before, although much dissipated, still lurked inside the house.

'Come with me, girl,' he called jovially from the door. 'I'm just going over to the *kraal* to cure Simon and the others.'

Oh, yes. There were others now, of course. The story of Simon's stomach complaint, and the boss's lenient approach to his problem, had gone round. There was some half dozen down with it.

Simon Sekubu was the first to be given the cure, as befitted the man who first claimed the complaint. As my uncle entered the *rondavel* with his evil smelling pot, Simon's family scuttled out behind him. He gave a low chuckle that only his daughter could hear, and approached the bed of the patient. Simon appeared to be sleeping but as the horrible smell wafted into his nostrils his eyes suddenly flew open.

'Time for your medicine, Simon,' Grandfather was at his cheerful best this morning.

He didn't play by halves, and the huge spoon he produced made the black man's eyes open even wider, until only the whites appeared to be showing.

One full spoonful later and my grandfather and his black pot moved on, leaving behind the sounds of much retching and moaning.

Six spoonfuls later and my mother followed my grandfather back to the house, where he sat on the *stoep* and drank tea. The black pot had gone back on the stove to simmer, for he had promised his patients another dose at noon.

'Four doses a day for three days,' he had told each of the bedridden men. 'And you'll soon be on your feet again.'

In the event, it was a miracle, and Grandfather was looked upon as a great *sangormo* long afterwards. For by twelve noon every one of the constipation sufferers had managed to stagger into the fields. Not that they did a lot of work that day, for now they had a slight problem that was the reverse of the original complaint.

Early the next morning Sammy Sekubu left the *kraal*, nursing bruises and sore parts administered by several of the women, who did not approve of their menfolk malingering.

Thereafter my grandfather's doctoring was largely confined to the standard phrase that, 'often the cure is worse than the complaint.' At these words his erstwhile patients usually fled back to their work, leaving him puffing his old pipe and smiling to himself.

'That too was very good, Michael,' the old man chuckled. 'I would like to have met your grandfather. He sounds a very good and wise man.'

They turned in for the night, and the young boy was relieved. He needed time to compose his memories of another story he'd once heard. Now he was on a roll and wanted to be a part of this story telling. Not once had he stammered or stuttered during either of the two stories he'd told, whereas if he'd been in class he could never have got through the first one.

'You know,' he said softly, as though to himself. 'I haven't even missed the television once. What a waste of time it is.'

Next to him the old man smiled, for he knew what was going through the boy's mind. He loved him, as he would have loved his own son if he had seen him grow from a new-born babe like the white boy.

One day he would grow into a fine man, and he felt a pang of empathy with his father, for he too had missed the best years of his own son's life.

'But there's a big fence going off in both directions,' Michael complained next day.

'That is the Giant's Castle Game Reserve,' Kqwedi told him. 'We have talked of the killing of the animals, and now they must be kept behind wire. It is to keep the poachers out as much as to keep the animals in.'

'We learn about it in school. The teachers call it ecology and conservation. Did you know there are only 5,000 tigers left in the whole world?'

'That is very sad,' the old man shook his head. 'I have seen pictures of them. They are beautiful animals, much bigger than the leopard, which the first Whites called the tiger. Now, we should go around this place.'

'Can't we just go across it? We could climb the fence easily enough. Or are you worried about the animals? I read that the only predators are leopard, *serval* and *caracal*. Oh, and there are jackal and baboon.'

The grizzled head shook again. 'No, Michael. It is not the animals we would have to worry about, but people. Many visitors come to look at the wildlife, and there are hiking and horse trails all over it.'

'Then we will have to avoid them,' the boy declared. 'It will take a lot of kilometres off our journey. If we need to we can sleep during the day and move at night.'

The old man smiled but did not comment on the lack of wisdom in moving at night. He nodded and the boy scampered over to the fence in delight.

They found a place where the wire could be easily lifted at the bottom, and they pushed their bags through and crawled after them. Away to their left the high pinnacles traced the skyline in splendid isolation, and to the south a great bastion rose above them all. This huge mass, connected to the main escarpment by a narrow *nek*, is one of the corner-stones of the Drakensberg, swinging the range from north-west to south-west, and is one of the highest points of the Berg.

'Giant's Castle,' Kqwedi pointed a gnarled finger. 'The Zulu name is *Bhulihawu* - the place of the shield thrasher - or *Phosihawu* - the shield flinger. It is named after a famous warrior of my people who had an unusual fighting style. He carried a small round shield, the edge of which was made of ironwood, sharpened and fire-hardened. He would fling it at the legs of a foe, with such strength that it would sometimes sever a limb, and render him helpless while Phosihawu moved in with his spear.'

Michael stared at the distant feature, and from the books he'd read he could imagine the wild glory of the tumbled mountain peaks and the mysterious untrodden valleys that lay there.

'My people say it is the birthplace of storms. Round its tops the clouds gather and the thunder roars, like the thrashing of a mighty shield, as Phosihawu would do to frighten his enemies. The great storm clouds are flung out across the waiting lands as one flings a shield, and the storm begins to move over the plains of Natal. The Bantu who ruled the land before the Amangwane called it *iNtabayikonjwa* - The Mountain At Which One Must Not Point - for the mountain resents being pointed at, and it makes bad weather. It is possible that both stories are right.'

The boy looked at the far-off mountain with a nervous expression on his face.

'Don't worry, Michael,' the old man laughed. 'There are no storm clouds today, and by tonight we will be up there among the rocks, where we will find shelter. We must be careful to avoid others, so keep watch around you.'

As they trekked across the open land, heading both northwards and towards the mountains, the old man would pause occasionally to gather something from the ground. Varieties of grass heads, ferns, leaves and young shoots disappeared into his bag. Sometimes he would dig up roots and bulbs.

Once they came across a flattened area of *veldt*, and with a suggestion that the boy could rest, he disappeared in the low ground to the right. He returned some time later with a huge grin and his bag looked considerably heavier to the intrigued youngster.

There were no more pauses after that, and they continued to move cautiously through the rest of the day, keeping a wary eye out. Once they saw a small group of moving figures in the distance but the old man smiled and said *'elandt'* in a low voice, and when they drew nearer Michael saw that they were indeed eland. Because of their excellent eyesight they were unable to get much closer before they were spotted. The group stood quite still for a few moments, all heads turned in the direction of the intruders, before they took off at a brisk trot.

It was the first time that Michael had seen eland, and although he knew it to be the biggest of the African antelope, he was still surprised to see it was the size of a large ox.

He was even more surprised when Kqwedi told him the Drakensberg eland was almost half the size than in other parts of Africa. Later in the day they saw *oribi* and grey *rhebok*, and as the shadows of the peaks lengthened, baboons could be seen on the higher ground, the males vocalising a warning with their loud bisyllabic bark.

Kqwedi followed a trickling stream up into a small lush valley, at the head of which was a collection of huge rocks that had tumbled from the heights centuries ago. They found an ideal spot alongside the water, surrounded by the grey sentinels of stone. The old man lit a small fire in the shelter of an overhang and then began preparing their evening meal.

He put the seed heads into a scrap of cloth and threshed them against a rock, blowing away the chaff when he was satisfied. Using the haft of his knife he pounded the seeds into fresh flour, and with water and the last of their cooking oil, he baked a small loaf.

The pot was put on to boil, with roots and bulbs, ferns, and the inside of a spiky plant that Kqwedi said was like spinach. Leaves and young shoots were added, and the last of their meat chopped up and thrown in. With a flourish the old man produced two large sweet potatoes and a couple of bananas. The potatoes went onto the embers at the edge of the fire.

'Where on earth did you get those?' Michael asked.

'The flat land where you rested this afternoon,' the old man chuckled. 'It was the site of a *kraal*, abandoned long ago. I knew they would have planted towards the river, and found these growing wild.'

He rose and began to root in his old leather bag. 'Now, tend the cooking Michael, while I lay a few traps for tomorrow's food.'

As the ancient warrior disappeared into the gloom of evening, the boy began to stir the mixture in the pot, smiling to himself in the knowledge that part of his goal had been achieved.

For tonight he would sleep under the protection of the Drakensberg Mountains.

The meal was excellent. When it was almost ready, the old man had returned and thrown in a handful of herbs, which produced a rich spicy flavour to the stew.

They ate the sweet potatoes separately and finished with mugs of strong hot tea. The sugar, like most of their rations, had run out, so they chewed the ends of the cane as they drank.

'How far off are we now?' the boy asked, though it was a reflex question only. He really didn't care whether it was a day, a month or a year. He was content, to sit here by the dying glow of their cooking fire, the sounds of the night coming alive around them. Whatever trouble he was in when he got back would be well worth it.

'Longer now than when we began,' came the roundabout answer. 'If we had kept a straight path, maybe two days. Now that we have chosen to follow the line of the hills, maybe a week or more. For me, it is the span of a lifetime.'

He watched in anticipation as the old man pulled out the battered old corncob pipe and began the lengthy process of cleaning and filling. Finally he leaned into the fire with a long twig and lit it, drawing smoke deep into his lungs.

He smiled at Michael, who returned the smile.

'Well, *jong*?'

'Well what?'

'You are forgetting. It is your turn to tell a story, my young friend.'

'Oh, yes. I did forget. I know the story of a climber. I heard my instructor telling it to some of the older boys one day. It's true, of course.'

'Of course,' the old man said gravely, enjoying the chance of a new tale.

The boy sat back, trying to recall the time he'd heard the story, and to his amazement it all came flooding back. Almost word for word, yet still he was unaware of the gift he had. The photographic memory that would prove his salvation when he returned to school.

CHAPTER TWELVE

THE CLIMB

Baldwin gazed up in awe at the Giant's Finger, outlined against a sky of radiant blue. Not a cloud marred the backdrop to the mighty rock, and nothing touched its outline as it towered a full 1000m above the valley floor. It took on the aspect of the Zulu name for the mountain range, and it did indeed resemble a spear, with the sun reflecting from its smooth surfaces.

Three-quarters of the way up an enormous overhang circumvented the entire feature, and above it the rock ran smoothly before tapering to a rounded top. From a closer stance this gave it the look of the appendage it was truly named after. Giant's Finger.

Baldwin took a deep breath, for he still found it difficult to accept that the dream of a lifetime was about to become reality. He had climbed every major peak in the Drakensberg, as had his father before him. But the difference was that his father had put up many of those climbs for the first time, something he himself had never done.

Not that he wasn't capable, people told him. These were climbing people who knew what his potential was, and without being unduly modest, he had to agree with them. It had to be admitted that Richard Baldwin was never unduly modest, not even any kind of modest, and even to his detractors he was one of the best climbers of his generation. He himself inclined to the view that he was one of the best climbers of ANY generation, but he unfortunately lacked the final proof of this.

A first ascent of a major climb.

Once you knew that a route had been climbed, the challenge went out of it. Of course the thrill and the excitement were there, but people remembered only who put up the first climbs.

His father had taught him to climb when a child, and as he grew bigger and stronger the quality and severity of the climbs increased. In his early twenties he could follow his father up anything. In his late twenties he could lead any climb in the Berg.

A few times he had gone overseas and climbed; the Llanberis in Wales, the Cairngorms in Scotland, and the Fells in England. Twice he'd climbed the Alps in Europe, and once he'd even spent a month in the Southern Alps of New Zealand.

But none of them meant the same to Baldwin, although he could not fault the quality of climbs that he found, nor the standard of the men he climbed with. His father had been a relatively poor man, and being unable to travel abroad he had climbed only close to home. This meant the Drakensberg, so for Baldwin to emulate his deeds he would have to find new ascents in his father's old stamping grounds.

His father had died when Baldwin was thirty-one, making it even more difficult to prove his superiority. He wanted to be recognised for himself, not to be forever known as the son of Mike Baldwin the climber. That thrill of vicarious popularity, gratifying when young, had now gone.

He was Richard Baldwin, climber in his own right.

He had long known there was one remaining bastion of the

Drakensberg's defiance, one last ascent that even his father had been denied from conquering, despite having tried many times. Always he'd been defeated, and a sympathetic climbing world and an understanding press were in accord. The Giant's Finger could not be climbed.

'Having second thoughts?' a quiet voice asked behind him.

Baldwin turned to look at one of his companions on the climb. Danie Breedt was the same age as himself, thirty-five, and was a grain buyer in Pietermaritzburg. He was well known as a good reliable climber, not averse to taking a risk now and then, but only after he'd weighed up the factors involved.

His steady approach to climbing would make up for the occasional irresponsibility of the third member of the team, Phillip Malan.

'Are you serious?' Baldwin replied with a question of his own, though neither required an answer. Baldwin's obsession with the Finger was widely known.

'You must know every inch of that rock better than you know your wife's backside,' Phil grinned up from making last minute adjustments to his gear.

Baldwin smiled without humour at the truth of the remark.

Over the past ten years he'd taken hundreds of photographs of the Finger, from every angle and using the finest cameras and lens. It had long been agreed that the best route was on the western side, the side his father had made three attempts at. He'd also tried other routes, but the west was his preference, though still without success.

Baldwin agreed on this, for he had flown over, and around, the feature many times, snapping away with his camera and viewing it intently through binoculars from the helicopter. He'd spent hours studying the photos and today they were taking the western route, following a complete set of pictures that mapped it out, metre by metre.

They had camped overnight in order to make an early start, for the climb would take two days. Both Danie and Phil had helped with the finance of the venture, though neither was affluent and both had families to look after. Obsessive climbers, like surfers, did not gravitate to well paid jobs, owing to their tendency to take off at a moment's notice; when the mountain was calling, or the surf was up.

They had clubbed together, but it had been left to Baldwin to make up the considerable shortfall. After all, it was HIS burning ambition; HIS lifetime goal; HIS Quixotic 'quest'. For the others it was simply more of the same. A few days sport, only.

It was seven o'clock, and the sun was five hours from creeping over the tip of the Finger and assaulting the climbing face with its power. Baldwin planned to be up to the chimney by then, and they could take shelter inside from the noon heat, belaying on and even preparing a decent lunch if it proved possible. Of all the prominent features on the route, the chimney was the one they knew least about. Hidden in shadow, even with the afternoon sun shining directly on it, it curved inwards and was still an unknown quantity.

'Right,' Baldwin's voice was tight, and he gave the climbers' positive starting cry. 'Let's crack it.' Words like 'try, attempt, endeavour', did not find favour in the climbers' handbook.

'Aren't we waiting for the press?' asked Danie.

'No,' Baldwin snapped, the adrenaline building now, causing his arms to feel heavy and his neck to ache. In a few minutes he'd loosen up again, and the chemical that surged through his body would make him capable of doing that little bit more than his body was aware of. 'We can't wait around for a bunch of media fairies. They know what time I said, and we can't leave it any later. We don't want to climb with the sun dancing on our backs. They'll be along.'

Phil agreed, also eager to get started, and Danie gave a good- humoured shrug.

They hoisted their light packs and checked the outside of each other's gear, ensuring that straps were fastened and there were no 'danglers'; pieces of equipment which could catch on protruding rocks or shrubs. Danie read off the main contents list; each nodding in turn as the items they were responsible for came up.

This close to realisation of the goal that had driven him for so many years, Baldwin's impatience knew no bounds and he almost ran to the foot of the climbing face. The others followed amiably, well aware of the driving force contained in their companion's spare frame.

The first two pitches were easy, and it had been decided that Danie would lead the first, followed by Phil on the second. Baldwin would then climb through and take over for the rest of the way.

'Come on, Danie,' Baldwin attempted humour to conceal his eagerness to begin. 'See how far you get before you peel off.'

'Don't worry about me, Richard,' Danie grinned. 'Just keep an eye on Phil. He's the one most likely to fall on you.'

He tied a figure of eight in the end of the rope, clipped onto his karabiner, then moved it around to his back. He climbed easily and well, using pitons every three or four metres, clipping on karabiners and threading his rope through them. At the first few pitches pitons had been left by earlier climbers, and all he had to do was hammer them in firmly until the metal rang with a clear, bell-like sound, indicating it would take the weight of a falling man.

Phil had the middle of the rope around his shoulders, and fed out half to the No 1. If Danie fell, he would lie back on the rope and hold him as he dropped below the piton.

As the rope began to run to it's middle, Phil called the distance and Danie began to look for a belay. He threw two coils over a solid knob of rock, settled himself securely, and tugged on the rope.

'Taking in, Two,' he called, and took up the slack.

As the rope came tight, Phil yelled, 'That's me'.

'Climb when ready,' came back down.

Phil called 'Climbing', and began.

He passed Danie and carried on to lead the second pitch. He belayed onto the rock, while Danie brought up Baldwin, who went past him and then above Phil, until he had completed the third, and hardest, pitch. He then brought up the other two, who belayed nearby, and he continued up. From now on he would lead, which was the way he wanted it.

The way he'd always wanted it.

The other two had agreed, naturally. Apart from being the best man on the mountain, it was mostly his money that had financed the attempt on the Giant's Finger. Both had wondered privately how he'd managed that, being only a half partner with his brother-in-law in the hardware store that was his wife's family business. Business everywhere had been bad of late, and theirs was no exception.

As Baldwin led easily up the next pitch, his thoughts were on that very same subject. His hands and feet worked on their own now, as a separate part of him, and he found that they knew exactly what they were doing without too much hassle from his brain.

He'd hired choppers, bought cameras and new equipment, and made numerous trips to recce the climb. None of it had come cheap of course.

He'd taken money from the business; money that his brother-in-law knew nothing about, and which he would repay from the climb. He'd be able to write a book about it; the first man up the Finger. Maybe they'd even film it. There'd be TV interviews, and newspapers would want his story. He wondered which actor would play himself.

There was no end to the speculation running through Baldwin's mind as he hammered a bright new piton into a wispy little crack in the face.

He'd repay the mortgage too, of course. It was his wife's house, for Jane had been married before and it had been part of her settlement. As such she owned it outright, without a bond or mortgage. The way he persuaded her to sign it over in his name was a stroke of genius, he thought. The hardware store had always meant something to her, having been in her family for generations. Jane was aware of the state of business, so when he told her he'd have to show collateral to keep it going, she agreed to the transfer.

Then he took out a large loan against it with the finance company, though he'd pay it back when he'd reached the top. He'd pay it all back when he reached the top. The wages from the safe, the money he should have sent off to the suppliers. Everything. Yet in his heart, Baldwin didn't give a damn about the money or rewards. He only wanted to get there, to prove he was the best. To beat his father's legend.

'Are you alright, Richard?' He heard Danie's voice calling up to him, and realised that he was still holding on to the last piton he'd driven in. He shook his head and concentrated on his next move.

The route he'd chosen went up past a smooth forty-metre wall that lay outwards at an impossible angle. An overhang was one thing, but this was to be avoided.

'Traversing,' he called to the two below, then edged out to his right, moving slower than before, and driving in pitons at shorter distances.

When he'd gone past the bottom of the inverse slope he searched for a belay point to bring the others across. The best he could do was to wedge a nut in a tiny crevasse. Taking a bight of the rope, he threaded it through the wire the nut was attached to, and thin though it looked it had a breaking strain in excess of 1000lbs.

As a back-up he threw a sling over a knob of rock that was out of reach, yet felt firm enough as he tugged on the sling, which he then hooked onto his harness. Danie came across the traverse and changed belays with Baldwin, who began the next pitch. The face was harder now, and the holds more elusive, and it took all his considerable skill at layback to get up a twenty metre crack.

He belayed on and called down, 'Two bring up Three,' and heard Danie reply, although now he could see neither of the other climbers. Phil was halfway across the traverse when it happened.

He was taking it too quickly, a fault of his when he was last man. Two had gone before so he found no challenge, no risk. Instead of testing each hold anew he moved on two points instead of the safety of three, and he was moving both his right arm and leg at the same time when the rock his left foot was balancing on came away from the cliff. His left hold was literally only fingertips, and not strong enough to take his body as the entire weight came on to them.

He managed to call out 'Hold', and his fall was checked by Danie within two metres, but the shock was enough to tear out the next piton, and Phil dropped another couple of metres, swinging out from the cliff and smashing back hard against it.

His howl of pain could be heard by Baldwin, who queried the situation in a loud voice.

'It's his elbow, Richard,' Danie called up to him. 'He peeled and a piton pulled out. He hit the face and I think he's broken something.'

Baldwin's curse carried down the cliff and he made an instant decision. 'Take him back down, Danie. I'll untie.'

'Don't be stupid, man,' came the reply. 'We can't carry on now. We need to get Phil down.'

'No,' came the shout from above. 'WE can't, but I can. I'm not bloody giving up now, for God's sake.'

'But you can't climb without protection, man,' Danie pointed out. 'You'll be free climbing the rest of the way.'

'Untying,' Baldwin ignored his pleas, and began to undo the end of the rope from his belt. 'Below,' he called, and the rope snaked down to the side of his No 2.

'Mad,' Danie muttered angrily. 'Completely bloody mad.' He called to Phil, then began the laborious task of lowering him the extent of his half of the rope.

Baldwin had already gained another ten metres when Phil had managed to belay himself below, and by the time Danie had retrieved Baldwin's end of the rope and changed his belay, the lone climber was entering the chimney.

He took a last look out across the *veldt* that swept away from him towards the west. The exposure was immense on this face of the Giant's Finger, but it was something Baldwin relished. The feeling of standing on an uncovered feature, with nothing to obstruct either the view or the feeling of empty space below his feet. It was his greatest turn-on. More euphoric than any drug could ever be.

He caught the flash of sunlight on something below and saw that several more vehicles now stood beside their own. He was pleased that the press had finally turned up. They would be taking pictures of him now as he continued his solo climb to the top, and he wouldn't disappoint them.

He disappeared into the chimney and looked up. It ran for about thirty-five metres, wide at the bottom and narrowing after the first ten, and this he could climb easily by bridging, bracing his back against one wall and his feet against the other.

Before that, however, he had to get up there. The left-hand wall seemed to be the more moderate and he started right away. It sloped outwards at the start, and he had to find secure grips for his hands, rather than holds, for at more than one time he had to swing his feet over to a more convenient spot.

By the time he'd gained the narrow part of the chimney, and begun the arduous but less skilful task of bracing, his companions were down again. Phil had managed to belay himself and untie the rope, while Danie pulled it back up and threaded half through the wire, making his own descent on the doubled rope. When he reached Phil he belayed again, and lowered his friend down to the bottom, then repeated his abseil technique.

By the time Baldwin had reached the top of the chimney, Phil was on his way to hospital to get his elbow set. They would return to spend the night in the tent, while the reporters and photographers would sleep in their vehicles, thus ensuring that all would be on hand to witness the terrible tragedy the next day.

A tragedy witnessed by many, but preventable by none.

Baldwin had one more pitch to go before he came to the overhang, and by now he could feel the powerful rays of the sun eating through his thin shirt. The small climbing pack kept the heat off, but pools of sweat formed beneath it. The pitch was not as difficult as he'd thought from the photos, though without safety measures he took it slowly. He knew that what he was doing was dangerous, perhaps madness as Danie had said, but that was no reason to be reckless.

Recklessness came on the overhang, when he moved out underneath the massive rock formation. Tiredness crept in and he should have rested, but denied himself, pushing his body to the limit. He was now using all his mechanical gear; strangely shaped pitons, tri-cams, friends, micronuts and rollernuts, small ladders, longer slings. All of which he'd carried with him from the start.

He would hammer in a piton, or fix in a friend or nut, then clip on a karabiner and long sling, into which he'd slip a foot to take his weight. Then another, and so on under the overhang. It was backbreaking work because it meant hammering above his head, neck stretched back, shoulder muscles aching.

He was three quarters of the way out from the back wall, and the sun had sunk low on the horizon, as though it had dipped purposely to peer in at him.

By now Baldwin was close to exhaustion, and he finally acknowledged that it was time to rest for the night. He took a climbing hammock from his pack and clipped it between two of the pitons. Next he pulled out a small object the size of a wallet, which unfolded into a silver space blanket. He spread this on the hammock and climbed on top, wrapping it around him to retain body heat.

He ate sandwiches and sipped glucose juice before falling into an exhausted sleep.

Baldwin spent a restful night, woken only once by the high-pitched, stuttering howl of a black-backed jackal, surprisingly close on the grassland below. He grinned nastily as he thought of the fright the press people would be getting in their cars.

With the dawn came a new sense of purpose. Once he was over the bulge of the overhang the rest was easy, with a shallow angle of ascent and good rock.

He ate a bar of chocolate and munched on an apple, aware that he had to top up with carbohydrates but despising his body for its time- wasting needs. Within a couple of hours The Dream would be realised, and he would be standing on the top of the Giant's Finger, the one climb his father had never been able to do. The climb that NO-ONE had been able to do. Until now.

He left the hammock and blanket where they were and began the tricky manoeuvre over the bulge. The hardest part was getting over the lip, and he achieved this by driving double pitons as close to the edge as he dared without breaking off a portion of the lip itself. He clipped a long sling between them that ran around his back, and he'd left a tape on the next piton back to support his legs.

He now lay on his back, facing the ceiling of the overhang, with his head just poking out below the lip, and reached out with both arms to drive in a piton above the outer rim of the lip. He clipped on a sling and was able to shove his left arm and shoulder through.

He moved his legs to the sling on the double pitons, moving them back until his feet rested on this, and he was able to push with his feet and pull with his left hand. Slowly his head and shoulders emerged above the lip and over the start of the bulge.

If Baldwin heard the single gasp from the watchers below, he made no sign. Nor could he, having now found a solid hold with his right hand so he could slowly begin to draw his body up and over the curve. His left leg came from the shadow below and the foot desperately sought the head of the piton.

This achieved, he was able to seek above him for more holds, gradually working his feet up and using them to push his body on, then his hands did their turn at pulling. And so it went. Finally he was able to walk on fingers and toes, until at last gravity told him to raise the front part of his body, for now the ground below him was flat. He'd made it.

Baldwin stood on the small plateau of rock and scrub at the top of the Giant's Finger. The first man to climb it, and his joy was so great that he cupped his hands to his mouth and yelled with all his might, and his friends below echoed it across the *veldt*.

A helicopter would soon be arriving to take him off, just as Danie had arranged the night before, followed by a triumphant interview with the eager newshounds, and Baldwin would return to Durban and his long-suffering wife. His dream fulfilled.

Which was why no one could understand what happened next.

An object was thrown by Baldwin and came hurtling down from 2000 metres above, miraculously missing the Channel I news team. Before anyone could move to inspect it, a cry came from the man on the Finger. This time it had the quality of despair, though none of the onlookers could make out the words.

Only Danie did. Later. For the moment he was simply one of the crowd, staring upwards in horror and disbelief at the figure of their friend, plummeting towards the ground. Time seemed to stand still to the watchers below, as he turned over just the once before landing among the rocks. At the foot of the climb that had been his life's ambition.

Most of the reporters had gone now, along with the Police and the ambulance.

'What did they need an ambulance for?' Phil asked bitterly. 'A bucket would have done as well.'

They sat around the fire that had been lit as the cool breezes began to drift down from the high Berg.

A local reporter from the town weekly had stayed on, generously sharing the bottle that he'd brought, and they were joined by the helicopter pilot who had turned up just minutes too late.

'You see, Richard's dream had become an obsession,' Danie was saying. 'And he wasn't too particular what he did to make that dream come true, as you saw when he left us to it and carried on by himself.'

'Yes, I know all that,' Phil said impatiently. 'But I still don't see why he threw himself off. He'd made it, he was the first man to the top.'

Danie shook his head. 'Not as far as he was concerned. He didn't give two cents for the money he was going to get out of it, or at being able to pay everything back. That wouldn't have caused him to jump. It was the thought that he'd failed.'

'But how did he know that?' Phil passed the bottle to the pilot. 'How did he know someone had beaten him up there?'

'What was that object you picked up, the one that he threw down just before he jumped?' Danie asked softly.

'An empty Coke can,' came the puzzled reply. 'But what has that to...?'

'Did you ever know Richard to drink Coke?' Danie asked patiently.

'No. You mean...'

Danie nodded. 'He obviously found it up there. Which explains the words he yelled just before he leaped. I caught '...here before', but it didn't mean anything at the time. Can you imagine what was going through the poor oke's head when he saw that can just lying there...?'

No one answered, for they were filled with their own thoughts. Especially the pilot, who was staring fixedly into the fire, and remembering a conversation he had only the week before. He'd been taking a friend up in a light aircraft, and the friend had thrown something out of the window.

'Litterbug,' the pilot had remonstrated.

'Bloody good shot,' his friend replied with a laugh. 'Right on the top.'

'You're still a litterbug,' the pilot had returned his laugh. 'It'll annoy some poor sod, man.'

'Nonsense,' his friend replied. 'That was the Giant's Finger, and you know as well as I do it's unclimbable. So who will ever see it to be annoyed, smart-ass?'

They had both laughed then.

But, in retrospect, the pilot wished they hadn't.

CHAPTER THIRTEEN

'Very good again, Michael,' the grey head dipped and his eyes sparkled in the faint glow of the embers. 'I did not understand much of the language of climbing but the story is very good. I think it is what the Whites call "black humour". I once saw a film about a Bushman who found a Coca-Cola bottle.'

'THE GODS MUST BE CRAZY,' Michael nodded. 'I think I saw it when I was very young, but I can't remember much about it.'

The old man tapped his pipe gently against the rock. 'The man who made the film was trying to show that a simple thing, not seen before by a simple people, could become an object of envy and the cause of much trouble.'

The boy thought about this for a while, and nodded slowly as he began to comprehend. 'You should have been a teacher, Kqwedi. You're not boring like some of mine, and you're easy to understand.'

The old man smiled. 'It was about a little Bushman who found an empty Coca-Cola bottle. Like your story, this too was thrown from an aeroplane and landed unbroken in the sand of the desert. Because of its shape, and its feel, his people thought it was a magic thing from the Gods. It caused jealousy and bad feelings among the tribe, and you must know the Bushman to understand what a terrible thing this was.'

The boy started as a nightjar's 'chookchookchook...' came from close by, changing to a bubbling 'poipoipoipoi...' as it took flight. The old man did not move.

'The Bushman, because of his constant movement, has few possessions. His weapons, sleeping skins, cooking pots, and the women's digging sticks, are all he needs. They share everything they have with each other, and no one wants what another has. So when this object of great desire came upon them, it changed their way of life. Fighting and arguing broke out among them, until finally the one who found it was given the task of getting rid of it.'

This time Michael took no notice as the 'hu-hoo' of a male eagle owl was answered by the 'hu-hu-hoo' of his mate. The old man smiled approvingly.

'But where could they get rid of such a valuable thing? To break it would be unthinkable, for it surely came from the Gods, and to leave it behind, or bury it, would be to invite someone else claiming it. There was only one answer.'

He calmly sucked on his pipe, eyes hooded against the rising smoke from the bowl, and seemingly unaware of the increasing sounds as the night creatures began to stir.

'It would have to be thrown off the edge of the world, for all Bushmen know the world is flat, and then no one could have it. The little Bushman set out and had many adventures as he searched for the edge of the world.'

'And at the end I suppose he realised that the bottle was just another part of the white man's civilisation?'

'No,' the old man's eyes were twinkling now. 'He did not go into the centres of civilisation, like towns and cities, but saw things only from afar. He was still convinced of the power of the bottle, and did the only thing he could do.'

'Which was?' the boy's impatience made Kqwedi smile openly.

'He found the edge of the world and threw it off, of course.'

For a few moments Michael stared at him, then the old man began to chuckle. He held his hand up finally in the sign of peace.

'He came to the edge of a huge cliff, with clouds swirling below him, and he thought that surely this must be the place. He threw it over and returned to his people, unchanged by his quick look at the world outside the desert, and his people stayed as simple as they always were.'

The boy chuckled softly, and they discussed the little Bushman and his precious Coke bottle, until his lids began to feel heavy and they turned in for the night.

They moved at a steady pace over the next few days. The old warrior wanted to finish the journey, and stopped less often. The boy was happy simply to plod along in his footsteps and gaze up at his beloved mountains.

There were animals and birds that he'd seen only in school books, yet they were a mere three hours by car from his home in Durban.

The old man took everything in his stride, for his interest lay to the north, and he was anxious to be in the country of his birth. Only once did he stand still and gaze heavenwards, as a giant shadow fell across them.

Michael looked up in awe at the bird gliding slowly above their heads with arrogant confidence, as though it knew they meant it no harm. It had a wingspan of nearly three metres, and its wedge-shaped tail was very long. The wings tapered backwards in flight and were night-black with streaks of white beneath. In contrast the white head, with pirate patches around the eyes, gave it a vulture-like appearance, which contrasted with its grace in flight.

'A bearded vulture,' he breathed softly, remembering his schoolwork. 'It's a link between the vulture and the eagle, with the feeding habits and feet of one, and the flight and beak of the other. I never thought I'd ever see one. Our teacher said they're very rare.'

'They are,' the old man agreed. 'Farmers shot them when they saw them standing over dead sheep, thinking they had killed them. But they are eaters of carrion, and do not kill. The *lammergeier* is sacred to my people and they say when the last one leaves the mountains, the Ngwane will soon be no more.'

'This is the only place in the world where they are found now,' Michael found himself saying. 'They are nearly extinct, though a long time ago they lived in Europe, the Himalayas, China and Arabia. Once one was seen over Mount Everest, soaring at the greatest recorded height of any bird.'

'I did not know that,' the old man said. 'Though it shows that my people were right in regarding such a bird as possessing mystical powers. Come, we have some way to go before darkness.'

In the late afternoon, as they were considering different places to camp, Michael pointed out a light shining through the trees of a small wood.

'Maybe it's the rest huts belonging to the Parks Board,' he suggested in a low voice.

The old man shook his head. 'No, the huts are further back. We passed them when we crossed Bushman's River. Remember we talked of the pass of Langalibalele, up to our left, and about the rebellion between his Amahlubi and the troops.'

'Then who can that be down there?'

'Maybe someone camping, Michael, but we must avoid them or they will pass on the news of our presence here. We will have to make some distance before we can stop for the night.'

They continued, but more cautiously now. They hadn't gone far when the old man stopped, hand upraised. The man and boy sank down on their haunches, and moved slowly forward through the low bush.

It was still light enough to see clearly. In a small patch of open ground a man was bent over a trap, from which he was taking a hare. He straightened, and held his prize up in both hands. The crack as its neck was broken carried across the still air to the watchers in the bush, and the boy couldn't help a little shudder running through his spare frame.

'*Vader, vader*,' the high voice came from behind them, and they turned to see a small girl watching them with big round eyes. 'There is someone here.'

The man dropped the hare and reached for a rifle lying next to the trap.

The boy stood up quickly. 'Please, mister. It's all right, we don't mean you any harm. My name is Michael, and this is my friend Jos...Kqwedi.'

'Come out,' the man ordered. He was a big man, though not fat, and he had the weariness of hard work about him. The rifle was old, but well cared for, and he held it like a man who knew how to use it.

'Move slowly, *jong*,' the old man said, stepping into the clearing and keeping his hands away from his body.

'You speak the *taal*?' the man asked.

'A little. My English is better.'

The man nodded. He examined them closely and relaxed visibly. 'You're not rangers.' It wasn't a question.

'We are travellers,' Kqwedi said solemnly. 'We are going to the valleys of the Mnweni where my people live.'

'You are Amangwane?'

'Yes. I left many years ago, and I return to lay down my head.'

This was an expression meaning it was the place he would die in. The man understood and nodded again.

'And the boy?'

'He is the son of my employer, and he is my friend. He goes with me to meet my people, and to see the mountains of the Drakensberg that has long been his dream.'

The man did not ask if the boy's parents were aware of his long trek, and he lowered his weapon as the little girl ran up and threw her arms around his thigh.

'Perhaps we can offer you a hot drink,' he said. 'My name is Theo, and this is my daughter, Dolly.'

Without waiting for acknowledgement he began to pick up his gear, then led the way through the bush in the direction of the light they'd seen earlier.

Michael found it hard to believe his eyes when he saw the hut. He'd seen better in squatter camps on the television. A framework of branches supported a mixture of tarpaulin and plastic sheets. A line of drying clothing hung between two thorn trees, and a semi-permanent fireplace had been formed from river-rocks.

The camp was on the banks of a higher tributary of the Bushman's River, and their host pointed to a feature far above them. 'That is Popple Peak, third highest in the Berg.'

'You know this land, mister?' the old man asked, looking around him without expression.

'I was farming not far from here, near Estcourt. Two years of drought was too much for the bank, and they foreclosed after the last crop perished.' There was a bitter note in his voice as he added, 'The rains came a month after we were thrown out on the streets.'

Michael was appalled. People thrown out on the streets. White people. He'd heard his parents talking about such things but he'd paid no attention. The man was saying it was the same all over, the banks were ruthless, and he'd heard there were Whites begging on the streets of Durban. The old man nodded solemnly, and the boy remembered people holding signs sitting in West Street and Smith Street, but he'd paid no attention.

'Have you no family to go to?' the boy blurted.

At that moment the flap lifted on the crude shelter, and a woman came out. She was fair-haired and pleasant faced, and was holding a child even smaller than the girl.

'This is my family,' the man said. 'My wife, Marie, and my son, Frikkie. My wife's family disowned her when she married me, and my parents are long dead. It is a sad story, gentlemen, and I won't bore you with it, but what you see here is all the family we need.'

'Theo, where are your manners,' his wife remonstrated with him. 'Hold your son while I make tea for our guests.'

The incongruity of her words, as if she was back in her farmhouse entertaining the Ladies' Guild to afternoon tea, made her husband and the two travellers smile, though there was sadness in the boy's eyes as they roved around the shabby campsite.

They sat on logs near the fire while she bustled around brewing in an old blackened pot, and proudly produced chipped pottery mugs. Holding the child her husband disappeared into the hut and returned with a half bottle of Klipdrift. When the tea was ready he poured good measures of the brandy into two of the mugs and handed one to Kqwedi.

'For the cold,' he smiled, for it was the old Boer excuse to drink brandy.

'For the cold,' the old man toasted, and they touched their mugs lightly together.

'Aren't you cold, Michael?' the woman showed concern at his nakedness. 'You have hardly got anything on.'

'I'm fine thank you, *mevrou*,' he replied, remembering his school Afrikaans. 'I'm used to it now. We warriors have to be tough, you know.'

'We know,' the man smiled.

It was still not dark, and they drank their tea and talked with the ease that strangers often have with each other, knowing they would probably never meet again, and the words they spoke did not have to be carefully picked over, as one tends to do with friends.

Michael spoke of his fondness for climbing, and his ambition to complete all the famous climbs in the Drakensberg. He rattled off the names; Devil's Tooth, the Column, the Rockeries, Outer Mnweni Pinnacle, Western and Eastern Triplets; and would probably have gone through all the lesser climbs in turn if Theo had not interrupted.

'Why have you not come here with your climbing club?' the ex-farmer asked.

He then found himself telling them of his father's opposition to his sport, and the frustrations he felt because of his poor showing at school.

The old man then spoke, in a few simple sentences, of his desire to retire to the land of his birth, and not to *kwaZulu* where they would build him a small house of brick. He mentioned his regrets for the departure from his village earlier in his life, following the death of his beloved wife.

'I am making a stew from this hare,' the woman called from the frail table she was using as a kitchen. 'There will be plenty for all if you will join us.'

The old man and the boy looked at each other. They knew the one little hare would scarcely feed the family alone, but they also knew that to refuse the generous offer would be an insult to the Afrikaners, who had a long history of courtesy to strangers.

'Only if you will allow us to add to the pot,' the grey head dipped. He delved into his bag and produced roots, herbs, green mealies, and sweet potatoes.

'We found the site of an old *kraal*,' Michael said expansively. 'So we knew they would have been some cultivation near-by, and these are what we found. Well, Joseph did, anyway,' he added honestly with a grin.

'Joseph?' the farmer raised his eyebrows.

'I was called Joseph by my employers, but now I have taken back the name given by my father.'

The man nodded. 'The food is welcome, game has not been easy to catch. I cannot use the rifle because of attracting attention.'

'What are you doing here?' the boy asked. 'Are you planning to stay for good?'

'No *jong*,' Theo smiled. 'We lived with friends at first, but they too were going through bad times, so we left early one morning. We decided to make our way across country to the Berg, where we were hoping to find work at one of the tourist camps. We are prepared to do anything. But about two weeks ago Frikkie became ill. While the others stayed here, I carried him to the nearest road, and hitched back to Estcourt. The doctor gave him some medicine and we've been here since.'

'He's looking better now,' Michael said.

'Yes, we'll be moving on soon.'

'I will see what I can do about more meat before it grows too dark,' the old man picked up his bow and vanished into the bush alongside the river.

While he was gone the woman prepared the food, her husband bounced his son on his knee, and the little girl moved shyly up to Michael. He smiled at her but she wouldn't come any closer to him. A thought struck him and from the side pocket of his rucksack he produced a small bag of jellybeans.

'My standby rations,' he grinned at the man, and stretched his arm out towards the girl. 'Here you are, Dolly, these are for you.'

She cast an enquiring glance at her father, who smiled and nodded, then she crept forward and hesitantly took them.

'*Baie dankie*,' she gave him a shy smile, and gazed at the bag with round eyes.

She opened it and took one out, looked at it for some time then walked across and gave it to her little brother. He snatched it greedily and pushed it all in his mouth at once, then looked at his hands to see where it had gone.

They all laughed and the woman, who had paused from her work, looked at Michael with a grateful smile. 'It has been a while since they had sweets,' she said quietly.

A short time later a dark figure came through the vegetation surrounding the camp, and the old man appeared with a big grin and a small buck around his neck.

'Oribi,' he said. 'I knew there would be a watering place along the river bank, and I was in luck.'

'Luck had little to do with it, friend,' the farmer said, lifting the buck off his shoulders. 'This was a very good shot through the top of the neck.'

'We will eat well tonight,' Kqwedi shrugged off the praise. 'The rest will last you a few days more.'

He won the resultant argument from the husband and wife by stressing the need for the children to have fresh meat, and pointing out that he and Michael would have no difficulty finding their own food. He tapped his bow significantly.

When the stew was ready, they ate it accompanied by the mealies and sweet potatoes. They sat and talked, and drank more of the hot sweet tea that the homeless couple seemed to have an abundance of. As they talked they watched the buck roasting over the fire, and later they would eat succulent slices of venison. By then the children would already be full and have been put to bed in the hut.

'Kqwedi has been telling me stories on our way here,' Michael said at one point. 'He's a very good story-teller.'

The old man laughed and pointed a finger at him. 'You are not so bad yourself, my little friend. He told me the tale of a climber, with such an end that I did not know if I should laugh or cry.'

'That is the best kind of tale,' Theo said in a serious voice. 'To be able to choose your own emotion when it is finished.'

'He's joking with me,' the boy pretended to sulk. 'Ask him to tell you about the Jakkalsberge. He swears it's true.'

'Would that be about the diamond?' the man asked innocently.

He looked at the old man, who looked at the boy, who in turn looked at the ex-farmer. They burst out laughing together, and the woman smiled tolerantly as the three males went into hysterical cackles and guffaws of mirth.

'You are an old fraud,' Michael said as the laughter subsided, and that set them off again.

'I only said I THOUGHT it was true,' the old man said eventually. 'And I never said it had not been told before.'

Which made them begin laughing once more.

Marie finally shut them up by producing the bottle of brandy and handing it to the old Ngwane, who took it with a nod, sipped and passed it to the younger man.

'As you have heard my story before, you must now tell one of your own, *meneer*,' he said gravely. 'But it must be true, of course.'

The woman shook her head as the laughter resumed.

'I must explain why my wife's people would not accept me,' the man said, and by his tone the guests at his fire knew the laughter had finished for the moment. 'I know the way they are, and I do not hate them for it, because I cannot understand it. My last name is Thompson, for my father you see, was an Englishman. Not South African English, like you Michael, but he came from the City of Liverpool, in England. He married my mother, who was from old Afrikaner stock. Unlike Marie's parents, they accepted him into their family.'

He paused, watching the old man pull out his old pipe and begin the ritual of cleaning, filling and lighting. His wife appeared at his side with an equally battered pipe and a leather tobacco pouch. He smiled at her and extended the pouch to Kqwedi.

'My grandfather fought in the war against the Boer, and was back here in the First World War. He told my father many tales of South Africa and that was what made him come out here. This story is also true,' he smiled.

CHAPTER FOURTEEN

THE PROMISE

Anfield is the home of Liverpool Football Club, and the stand at the supporters' end is known far and wide as the Kop. Many of the older fans might know that its full title is Spion Kop, but very few would be aware that its origin lies on the plains of Natal, during the Boer War in South Africa. In Afrikaans, *spioen koppie* literally means, 'spy hill', but it was also called 'Look-out Hill', for it was the place from which the *voortrekkers* first looked on the promised land of Northern Natal, during the Great Trek.

Lying to the north of the Tugela, Spion Kop is 1,470 feet above the river. Surrounded as it is by loftier neighbours, such as the Rangeworthy Hills, the Twin Peaks, Brakfontein, and Vaal Krantz, it seems insignificant today, especially if you were to gaze from Mount Alice across the five mile wide gorge of the Tugela River.

In 1900, however, the little hog-backed hill was of strategic importance, being the hub and natural strong point of the whole range. The British were moving northwards, and their commander, General Buller, had decided that it must be taken. Although it was so precipitous as to be the last place the Boers would expect an attack, it also commanded the wagon road needed by the British to march their supply wagons north.

On the night of the 23 January, the assault force crossed the Tugela and launched its attack on Spion Kop. It consisted of two thousand men; mostly from the three regiments that made up the Lancashire Brigade, and with two hundred irregulars of the Mounted Infantry and half a company of engineers.

By four in the morning of the 24th, and at a cost of only ten men wounded, Spion Kop belonged to the British, and the men began to dig in. But although they had gained the summit, the mist had made them stop on what was actually a false crest.

At about eight o'clock the mist began to clear from the peaks and the Boers began a counterattack. The battle raged all that day and late into the night, and although the British were cut to pieces by rifle and artillery fire, their heroic defence of the tenuous hold on the summit caused many casualties among the determined Boers.

By the time the moon rose it had ended, and over two thousand men on both sides had been killed, wounded or captured.

The battle had been observed from several different places. On the crest of Mount Alice the war correspondents, including a young man named Winston Churchill, complained about Press censorship and debated how THEY would do it if they were in charge. Buller was watching from his HQ, also on Mount Alice. The Boer Generals, Botha and Burger, were watching from THEIR HG behind Green Hill to the north.

There was one other person who listened to the sounds of man-made thunder, and watched the tiny ants disappear into the smoke and reappear on the other side, though fewer in number each time. He had a good vantage point, for he was sixteen feet above the ground repairing a broken vane on a windmill. The windmill supplied water for the small farm he lived on, which was located to the northeast of the battle. The farm did not belong to him, but to the people he worked for, an English family named Anderson. To escape the war they had gone to relatives in Durban, for their cattle and produce had been requisitioned by the Boer Army and they had nothing left.

To begin again would be a waste of time, for when the British passed through, they too would take what there was. They would, like the Boers, hand over requisition chits which could be cashed in after the war, but surely only the winning side would pay on them?

They had left behind half a dozen or so Zulu workers, paying them what was owed and telling them to return to their kraals, for there was nothing to do until the farmer and his family came back to run the farm once again.

This they had duly done, except for Albert Nzuzi. Albert had worked on the farm for many years, and through several different generations of Andersons. He regarded the place as his home, and indeed the farmer, and his father before him, had given Albert the run of things. Since they'd been gone, he had tried to tend the fields on his own, feeding himself from the tiny kitchen garden.

He shook his head sadly as he descended the ladder from the sight of battle in the distance. As a young warrior Albert had fought both the Boer and the English, and admired them for their bravery in battle and their superior knowledge of all things. He could not understand why such people, beloved by the Gods, would wage war on each other. He respected the Boer but he loved the English for he had worked for them most of his life, and they had been good to him.

All the next day and throughout the night the retreat continued, back to the British camp behind the flanks of

Mount Alice. It was a terrible night, pitch black and with driving rain lashing the defeated Britishers. Behind them the Boers were consolidating their position, and sending their prisoners back under escort.

Among these demoralised wretches was a young lieutenant by the name of Longdon. He had been shot in the left shoulder, but no medical aid had yet been available to him. Through the appalling night the prisoners stumbled along, those who were whole helping the wounded as best they could. Lieutenant Longdon refused all help and made his own way in the van of the party. The men of the Carolina Commando guarded the rear, and could hardly be blamed for failing to notice the lone figure who slipped off the track to the right, and lay hugging the ground as still as any of the rocks about him.

He lay there a long time, until he was certain that all of the Boers had gone past, then rose to his feet and staggered away into the night. The following hour seemed like days to the young officer, the pain of his wound making him delirious at times. Once he thought he saw a light to his right and he altered his course to strike for it, not knowing whether it was a figment of his imagination or not.

It was indeed real, and as he drew close he saw the darker lines of a small group of building silhouetted against the night sky. Not caring now whether it was friend or foe, he half-crawled to the smallest of them, the one with the light in the window. It was Albert's hut, for although he could have moved into the farmhouse when his Whites had left, he had chosen not to.

It was with some trepidation that he heard the faint knocking on the door, and he opened it fearfully. The bloody figure wearing the uniform of a British officer collapsed into his arms, and Albert supported him from falling on the hard packed earth and dung of his floor. He half-carried the wounded man and laid him on his own bed, which consisted only of a palliasse in the corner.

The old Zulu had seen many *assagai* and bullet wounds in his lifetime. He brought the rusty hurricane lamp closer and examined the young soldier's wound carefully. He knew that the bullet was still in there for he could find no exit hole, and he was also aware that it had to be removed or poison would set in.

Albert heated up an old spear head in his cooking fire, for although he had never heard of sterilisation, he had learned from the Whites that this must be done to fight off the evil spirits that can enter a man's body through unclean instruments.

When the hot metal first touched his flesh, Longdon fainted, and he knew nothing of the probing finger of the *assagai* as it searched for the piece of lead. At last the Zulu had it between his bloody finger and thumb, and he threw it into the fire with an entreaty to the Gods that with it the evil spirit would also be gone from the young warrior's body. He heated his spear tip once more and cauterised the raw flesh around the bullet hole. He then went outside to his tiny garden, returning with the necessary plants and tubers to make a strong poultice, and this he bound tightly around the Englishman's shoulder.

For twelve hours he sat by the side of the young officer, alternately squeezing water into his mouth with a damp cloth, or mopping his brow with the same. Late in the afternoon the fever left the wounded man, and he sank into a peaceful sleep. Albert prepared a thick broth of vegetables for when his charge awoke, then sat gazing thoughtfully into the fire, and dreaming of days long gone.

During the Zulu Wars of 1879 Albert had then been called Kumbeka Nzuzi, a young warrior in the uMcijo regiment, which was part of the great king Cetshwayo's vast army. He had fought at Rorke's Drift when the might of the Zulu Nation was hurled again and again at the tiny post with its few defenders. Cetshwayo, ever the wise commander, had not ordered the attack, and had in fact told the chiefs of his *iMpes* that they were not to go against Whites 'behind walls and with slits to fire out of'. But they had not listened, and Kumbeka Nzuzi had said goodbye to many friends that day. After twelve hours of fierce fighting, the Zulus had lost 500 dead to the defenders 17, and their wounded ran into thousands.

Later, at a hill named Isandlwana, the victory had been reversed. The British force had gone out from their camp at the base of the hill that seemed to rise from the plain itself, but this time they had left no walls with slits in them, nor even a single trench with which to defend themselves. The legendary horns of the Zulu *iMpes* closed in, formed of the famous regiments: the uMcijo, Nokenke, Nodwengu, inGobamakosi, uMbonambi, Undi, and the uDkloko. In all 20,000 warriors. Of the 1,200 defenders, only a handful were alive by the end of that day.

Albert sighed in remembrance of that great hour of Zulu glory, for it was to be short lived. Later he fought at Khambula and Gingindlovu, after which the Zulu army was broken for ever.

He started as he heard the sound of horses fast approaching from the west, the direction of the Boer's HQ. He adjusted the old blanket that covered the Englishman, pulling it up to cover the lower part of his face, and damped down the fire with handfuls of dirt.

Outside he waited for the riders with the lantern held high, his right arm well out from his side to show that he carried no weapon. As they reined up before him, he recognised the *feld kornet* as the one in charge of the foraging party who had visited the farm the week before. They had taken all the vegetables that he had, and had not bothered to give him the slips of white paper that his employer had always received in lieu of payment.

'Kaffir,' the *kornet* cried. 'Have you seen any of the Khakis go this way? They have been badly beaten by the

Afrikanervolk and are spread all over. There is a reward for the capture of any.'

Albert shook his head. 'No, *baas*,' he replied in the humble voice he used for certain Whites. 'No English this way, *baas*.'

The *feld cornet* wheeled his horse and cantered off at the head of his men. He was disgruntled, for so far the prisoner patrol had been a waste of time, and he cursed the captain who had sent him on this stupid task. Everyone but the captain knew the Khakis had fled back across the Tugela and there were none left in this area.

When the last hoofbeats were but an unpleasant memory, the Zulu re-entered his hut. He hung up the lamp and turned, to see the young officer staring up at him.

'Thank you,' he said softly. 'Thank you, friend, for all you have done for me. You have saved my life.'

The old black man nodded with dignity. 'You are welcome,' he said in the English tongue. 'Soon you will be ready to travel and I will guide you back to the *rondavels* of the Khakis.'

Most of that day the wounded man rested and regained his strength. He slept often, and each time he woke his rescuer was ready with hot broth. By evening he insisted he was ready to return.

Under the cover of darkness they set off from the desolate farmstead. The old Zulu had eyes that could penetrate the gloom, and the young English lieutenant trudged on behind him. Keeping Twin Peaks on their left it was but a mile and a half to the north bend of the Tugela, and they followed this down another two miles to the dogleg where the river swung back near Potgieters Drift, and nearly met itself.

Albert found a log, and with this to hold on to they crossed the river, swollen now by the incessant rains.

On the far bank it was less than two miles to Mount Alice, and General Buller's demoralised camp. The Zulu refused to go into the camp, and took his leave within sight of the first sentry position.

'I will find you again, my friend,' Ralph Longdon promised, gripping the callused hand of his benefactor. 'And you will be rewarded for what you have done for me. There will be a medal from my Queen when I have told of your courage in defying the Boers.'

Albert took his leave of the young Englishman, his heart filled with the promise of a medal from the great white Queen across the ocean. He had often seen the medals of the soldiers, and fine things they were. Bright shining discs with her own head upon them, hanging from cloth of many wondrous colours. The white men respected those who wore medals, and he, Albert Nzuzi would wear his with the same pride.

His young officer had made him a vow, in the name of his Queen, and he would not break it. Hadn't he told him that he bore the same name as the husband of the Queen, Prince Albert? Though why he was only a Prince, when his wife was a Queen was beyond the simple comprehension of the old warrior.

the weeks turned into months, and the months became years, but still Albert waited patiently for the day when an envoy would come to the lonely farmstead. A representative of the great white Queen, to give him the medal he was due.

He hoped that it would be the young lieutenant again, but he would not mind if he was busy elsewhere, fighting for his Queen in some other place.

Sadly, this was never to be, for ten days after their terrible defeat at Spion Kop, Buller's men were once more crossing the Tugela in retreat, this time leaving 333 dead and dying at the Battle of Vaal Krantz.

Among them was a young officer, Lieutenant Ralph Longdon, who was one of the first to fall. Later his parents would receive his posthumous VC for valour in leading his men in a gallant charge. He'd had no time to tell anyone of his escape and rescue. Nor of his friend, Albert, and his promise of a medal.

The long years rolled by, and the war eventually faded away, though it did not happen overnight. Even after the peace treaty was signed at Pretoria on the 31 May 1902, many Boers ignored it and fought on in their *Kommando* units.

The Andersons never returned to their farm, for they fell victims to cholera before they had even reached Durban. Albert remained there alone, tending his little garden and keeping a watchful, if unnecessary, eye on the farm. In late summer of 1912, just as his mealies were green and ready for picking, a family of Dutch immigrants found the farm and claimed it as their own. Being new to Africa they did not trust the Blacks, and drove the old Zulu away with only what he could carry on his back.

He travelled to his old *kraal*, where he lived with one of his many grandchildren. It was not too far away, for he had to be near the farm if his Englishman, or the Queen's representative, came to see him. He often walked over to gaze at the farm from a distance, and one day he saw that the Dutch people had left, for with little knowledge of the soil of Africa they had failed to wrest a living from it.

They had been there less than a year. Albert moved back in, replanted his garden, and waited patiently.

A year later, on the 14th August 1914, the British declared war with Germany, and on the 8th September, South Africa joined them. There was no argument about the decision to go to war, only about whose side they should be on.

Afrikaner Nationals made an abortive attempt to take over the country in support of their German friends, many of whom lived in South Africa. They had even fought alongside the Boers in the war against Britain, and the first shots on Spion Kop had been fired in reply to the challenge of *"Werda?"* (Who goes there?), from a German sentry.

The old Zulu, carefully tending his garden and awaiting that long-ago promise, knew nothing of these global events; nor would he have shown interest if he had. The consequences, however, were about to touch upon his simple life.

One morning he went to his door and saw a column of dust rising from far off on the road from the north. As it drew nearer he could see that it was a long convoy of khaki uniforms and trucks, and as they finally halted at the farm, he went out to greet them with a big smile on his face. The British had come back at last, and surely now he would get his medal from the white Queen across the water.

The soldiers of the new South Africa were using the farmstead as a training camp, and the old Zulu was taken on to look after the mess-hall and whatever other chores they could find for him. Many of the soldiers had come out with Buller's Army and had stayed on after the war. Now they found themselves back in uniform again and with wry British humour they laughed at the irony of it.

Albert would wander around peering into the white faces and asking for Longdon and telling his story. They laughed gently at him at first, then became used to having him around, clearing the plates in the mess tent, and taking away the beer bottles later. Someone always had tobacco for him, and often one of the English would give him a bottle of beer, but this was frowned upon by the Afrikaners. 'You is spoiling the *kaffir*, man', they would say, but they too would hand him tobacco or chocolate when their Brit comrades weren't watching.

Among these ex-Tommies, now new Colonials, were men from the ill-fated Lancashire Brigade who had fought at Spion Kop and Vaal Krantz. They were men from Liverpool and Manchester, Preston and Wigan, with big hearts and the Northern sense of what was right.

One night Private Arkright beckoned Albert over and made him repeat his story to his companions. After he'd gone back to his chores, one of the men looked thoughtful, then called to another table. 'Sergeant Holly, you was with the Fusiliers, wasn't you? D'you remember an officer named Longdon?'

'Aye,' the SNCO replied. 'Young lieutenant, good sort 'e wus. Wounded on the Kop, an' escaped arter 'e wus taken. He got it fur good at Vaal Krantz. Got a post humus VC, an' 'ighly deserved it accordin' to them what wus wiv 'im.'

He moved over to join them. 'I wus jus' a young private meself then. Wot's it about?' he asked, and they told him, all talking at once as was their way.

The following evening, when the mess tent was full of men drinking beer, playing cards and talking in loud voices, Sergeant Holly suddenly called for silence.

There was an immediate cessation of activities and the men waited expectantly.

'Bring in th' recipient,' barked the sergeant in his broad Liverpudlian tones, and Privates Arkright and Moore came through the tent flap escorting a bewildered Albert between them. When they drew near the makeshift bar, the sergeant stepped forward and addressed the old Zulu.

'Albert Nzuzi, fer your 'eroism an bravery, in savin' the life of one of our comrades, in the year 1900, I 'ave the 'onour to bestow upon you the Tommy Atkins Medal for outstandin' 'eroism 'an service.'

With a flourish, Private Arkright produced a cap badge hanging from a long length of ribbon. The badge was of the Lancashire Fusiliers, the regiment of Ralph Longdon. It had been dug out of the kitbag of Sergeant Holly, who had spent a long time polishing it up to its gleaming brightness.

A young soldier who had bought it for his sweetheart in Bloemfontein had donated the gaily-coloured ribbon.

As the ribbon was hung around his neck, old Albert felt his eyes well up with tears. 'It is from the Queen?' he asked softly.

'That's right, mate,' the sergeant nodded. 'Queen Mary 'erself.'

Albert had not known the name of his young officer's Queen, nor that she had died in 1901 and been replaced by her son, Edward. He too was now dead and there was another king on the throne of England, George. But as far as the old Black was concerned, neither the young Englishman, nor his Queen, had forgotten him.

There was no more work for Albert that night, and he sat at pride of place at the sergeants' table, where he was congratulated by his friends the Khakis. Some of them spoke Afrikaans, which he thought strange, but he had long ago given up trying to understand the ways of the Whites, and he now accepted things as they were.

When he slept that night the old man was content, for his dream had been fulfilled, his patience justified, and his hopes realised. He had his medal from the white Queen at last, and the next morning they found him with a peaceful smile on his face.

He had died sometime during the night.

His friends, the Khakis, buried him with full military honours, for he had become a symbol of more than a brave old man who had helped a young lieutenant.

With the death of the warrior Kumbeka Nzuzi, one time soldier in the uMcijo regiment of the great king Cetshwayo, so too had died another era in the stormy history of Southern Africa.

There were tears in the young boy's eyes when the man finished speaking, and his wife wept unashamedly, though she had heard the story before. Even old Kqwedi rocked backwards and forwards slowly, his black eyes glistening in the fireglow.

'I think the beast is done,' he said gruffly, and helped by the white man he took the buck off the fire and laid it on the table to cool. Later it would be salted and hung on the branch of a tree, out of reach of scavengers.

Strips were sliced off and they sat quietly eating the delicious flesh, alone with their own private thoughts.

'What did you mean by the end of an era, Mr Thompson?' Michael asked after a while.

'The end of lots of things, and the beginning of others,' the man said philosophically, then realised the boy deserved a proper answer. 'The simple life was over for most people, and the age of technology came in. The advances in medicine mean that people do not succumb to disease as they once did, and the human race is living longer. Since the Second World War we have been using up the resources of our planet at an ever-increasing speed and only now are some people beginning to care.'

'It probably began a lot earlier,' the boy said, remembering the old man's story of the time of the animals.

'It did,' Theo Thompson agreed. 'But at a slower rate, now things seem to be snowballing over our fragile planet. A bitch can only whelp so many times before she becomes barren, and her dugs milkless. A good farmer knows that what you take from the land must be replaced. Marie has a poem that expresses it all very well.'

'It is not a poem,' she corrected with a smile. 'More like a prayer. I read it years ago and memorised it because it was so beautiful, and so true.'

She sat at her husband's feet, and he stroked her hair as she began to recite in a clear voice, which the light Afrikaans accent did nothing to detract from.

'If the Earth was only two feet in diameter, floating above a field somewhere...

'The people would walk around it, marvelling at its big pools and its little pools, and the water flowing between them.

'The people would marvel at the bumps on it, and the holes in it, and they would marvel at the very thin layer of gas surrounding it, and the water suspended in the gas.

'The people would marvel at all the creatures walking around the surface of the ball, and the creatures in the water. The people would declare it sacred because it was the only one, and they would protect it so that it would not be hurt.

'The ball would be the greatest wonder known, and people would come and pray to it;

'To be healed,

'To gain knowledge,

'To know beauty; and

'To wonder how such a thing could be.

'And the people would love it and defend it with their lives, because they would somehow know that their lives, their own roundness, could be nothing without it;

'If the Earth was only two feet in diameter, floating a few feet above a field...somewhere.'

CHAPTER FIFTEEN

They slept in the open that night, for the sky was clear and they lay close to the fire.

Random thoughts were tumbling around in the boy's head, and confused as he seemed over certain issues, he was aware that no amount of schooling could make up for the things he'd learned on this trip.

He woke instantly at the touch on his shoulder, every sense alert, as is the way of the creature of the bush he was turning into. The old man beckoned and he followed obediently behind him. He did not need to dress, for his clothing was the simple loincloth he had slept in.

'The young ones will have eggs for breakfast,' Kqwedi told him when they were out of earshot of the camp. 'I will point them out and you will fetch them, for I am too old and filled with dignity to climb trees and enter cold water.'

Behind him Michael grinned to himself, for he knew the old man was capable of doing both at least as well as he could himself, but he would give in to his whim.

They were returning along the river bank, laden with duck eggs (only two from each nest as the old man had ordered) when Kqwedi stopped suddenly and stood still, head held up in listening stance.

'We must get back to the camp and warn them,' he said, and lengthened his previous pace. Mystified, the boy hurried after him.

By the time they reached the clearing Michael could also hear it, a faint drone away to the east. Drawing nearer.

'It is a helicopter,' the old man told the Thompsons. 'We must cover your shelter with branches, and hide everything.'

They worked quickly. Table and cooking utensils went into the shelter, the fire was put out and the stones scattered. The washing had been taken down the previous evening, but the long length of line was untied and coiled.

They all knew what would happen if they were found.

Apart from being trespassers in the game reserve, they would be arrested as poachers when the dead buck was discovered. Though it was nothing to what the professional poachers would take, and necessary to their survival, Theo said, the law still applied to everyone.

Branches and ferns were piled over the hut, especially the shiny surface of the plastic, and they hid inside as the 'clip-clip' of the rotor blades came nearer to their place of concealment. It passed almost directly above their heads, though without appearing to slow down.

'They are following the *Boesman's Rivier*,' Theo Thompson said. 'This way will take them to the higher Berg.'

'I think they're looking for us,' Michael said with a white face. 'My father must have hired it.'

'He must be worried about you, Michael,' the woman laid a gentle hand on his arm. 'You might not think so, but I'm sure he loves you very much.'

'We must leave,' Kqwedi said abruptly. 'We do not want them finding you by mistake.'

They all knew he was right, and a few minutes later they made their farewells. Marie Thompson insisted on wrapping a piece of the cold meat and slipped it into the boy's pack, and they would refill their waterbottles at the river as they crossed it.

They wished each other good luck, and the woman hugged them both in turn, much to the old man's embarrassment. Only the boy saw the pleased smile tugging at the corners of his mouth. It was Michael's turn to be embarrassed when the little girl, Dolly, threw her arms around him, and kissed him as he bent down to her.

The feeling of sadness remained with him for several hours, as they headed in a northwesterly direction, making for the head of the Little Tugela.

'The Zulu name is *Injasuti,* well-fed dog, because in the early days the game was plentiful in the area,' the old man said. 'Now they would go hungry, I think.'

The sun had long passed overhead when they stopped to eat some of the oribi meat, and slake their thirst at the second of the four tributaries of the river.

They continued on, keeping close in to the foothills, and matching the curves of the high country. No longer frightened by the other inhabitants of the Berg, Michael laughed as a particularly aggressive baboon, obviously a look-out for the troop feeding on the heights above him, began to strut his stuff and screamed abuse at the strangers passing below.

Two black eagles wheeled above them at no great height, with their characteristic narrow-based wings, and white flashes at the base of the primaries. They were silent, as was their way. Their courtship led them below the level of the two travellers, and the prominent white 'V' stood out on their backs.

Michael sighed, finding it hard to believe how alive he felt, how grateful he was to his old friend for showing him all this.

He kept glancing at the peaks high above, trying to work out routes, and guess which climbs could be where.

It was late afternoon when a sudden call made him look up once more, and he saw a figure waving frantically from a narrow outcrop of rock.

'Michael. Thank God I've found you,' the figure shouted. 'Stay there and I'll come down.'

'No,' the boy yelled back. 'Father, don't. Where you're standing...it's not safe. Get back, pleas...'

The cliff crumbled as he spoke, and began to move forward slowly, the whole edge sliding with the man's weight.

'Get back,' he heard the old man repeat his words but they were directed at him, not his father. He felt the gnarled fingers grab his arm, but he was unable to move, gazing with horror at the figure high above.

Kqwedi threw an arm around his waist and hurled him forward under the cliff, as rocks and boulders began to rain down upon them. The old man, his speed belying his age, dived after the boy beneath the overhang.

It lasted but a minute, and they ventured out expecting to see Michael's father lying amongst the fallen debris. A weak cry attracted their attention back up the face, and they saw him stretched out at a precarious angle some three to four metres below the top. Here the cliff had come away completely, leaving a sheer wall of rock above the stricken man.

'Mister Clements,' the old man addressed his employer by name, instead of the usual 'baas', for that was of the past now. 'How bad are you hurt?

'I...think my leg...is broken,' the feeble voice answered.

'You must...get help from...the rangers. I'm on a narrow ledge, but it's not...too safe.'

'There's no time to waste,' Michael said decisively, and the old man looked at him in surprise. 'The rest of that cliff could come down at any minute, or he could lose consciousness and roll off the ledge. I must go up and belay him.'

'But you have nothing,' Kqwedi frowned. 'I know little of climbing, but I do know that things are needed...'

The boy flung his bag on the ground and extracted a few items, rattling off names as he did so.

'I brought a few slings, karabiners, and a couple of rope hexcentrics,' he panted. 'Just in case I got to climb something.'

He saw the look on the old man's face, realising he didn't understand what he was talking about. 'What I didn't bring was a rope, which I don't have. You must go back to the camp and ask Mr Thompson for the rope he used as a clothesline. It wasn't too thick but there was a lot, so we should be able to double it.'

Kqwedi was still looking confused, as much at being ordered by the boy, as at the events that had caused such a turn-about to happen. But he was wise enough to know his limitations in this matter.

'I should stay here to watch for you, Michael. If you fall...'

'No, you must fetch the rope, my friend. I will belay us both to the cliff until you come back, then you and Mr Thompson can lower us down from above. Please, you must be quick, Kqwedi.'

The old warrior knew the boy was right, and he placed his bag beside the rucksack, grasped his bow firmly and turned back the way he had come.

He could not help pausing by the edge of the small wood they had passed through, and watched as the boy emptied his rucksack on the ground, then put back his sleeping bag, water bottle and the meat. He threaded the slings over his neck, clipped the karabiners and hexs on to them, and commenced climbing up to the ledge where his injured father lay.

He went up the first few metres easily, and that was all the old man waited for. He could bear to watch no longer, and set off at a fast walk through the trees, knowing that time was precious. They had been walking for a whole day, and he must cover that distance twice more before the stricken man could be taken down from his dangerous position. He began to pray, first to the God of the Whites, later to the old gods of the Ngwane.

After ten metres the climb became harder, and the boy had to call on all the skills he'd learned in his short experience. Small flake fingerholds, handjams, pinch grips, finger pockets, fistjams, undercuts, counterbalances, friction grips; anything and everything that would get him another hold higher, another few centimetres towards his father. He was spurred on by the occasional cries of pain, and he called back as often as possible in an attempt to keep him awake.

If he dozed off, and moved in his sleep, he could easily go over the edge...and be killed.

His arms were aching at the work they were being asked to perform, though his legs were in good shape due to the amount of walking he'd been doing lately. At one stage he went up a section using virtually his arms alone, and he was forced to insert a hexcentric nut in a small crack, then thread his arm through to rest. Thereafter he tried to conserve his energy, and not make any sudden or jerky movements. But it was not easy to do. He wondered vaguely if it had ever been climbed before, or whether he was actually putting up a new climb. Then he felt ashamed as he remembered what his purpose was, and gritted his teeth to concentrate on the task in hand.

At last he reached over a lip above his head, and instead of feeling rock, he touched the denim of his father's jeans. He mantled onto the ledge very slowly, taking care not to make any sudden movement to disturb anything.

'Michael, is that you?' his father murmured.

'It's me, dad. I'm going to belay us both. Hold on.'

He tried to ignore the blood on his father's face, and not to look at the odd way his lower leg stuck out. He found a chockstone - a small rock wedged into a crack - and threw a sling over it, clipping a karabiner into the two ends. He looped a longer sling under his father's armpits, and attached it to the karabiner.

Now his father was safe. He searched for another belay point, but had little luck until he moved along the narrow ledge, and saw a tight crack running up, concealed by a thin ridge of rock. With an effort he was able to wedge a small hex into it, and clip on a karabiner and sling, which he placed under his own arms.

'Right, dad,' he said, his voice filled with a confidence he didn't feel. 'Where does it hurt?'

The head wound looked worse than it was because of the blood, and was already congealing as he wiped it with a damp handkerchief. The leg was a different matter, and when he'd cut the trouser leg away he saw the white bone sticking through the skin.

'It's a greenstick fracture, I think,' he told his father. 'All I can do is tie both legs together to prevent any movement in the bad one.'

He used his belt and a spare sling to do this, securing the knots above and below the break.

'How do you...know about this?' his father asked.

'The climbing club,' he looked him straight in the face. 'The one you said I wasn't to belong to.'

'It's a good job you didn't listen to me then,' his father smiled weakly. 'Or you couldn't have saved my life.'

Michael did not reply, but held his father's head up carefully and tilted the waterbottle to his lips. He drank greedily, and the boy had to take it away before he emptied it.

'Thanks...Michael, and I'm sorry...'

'Sorry for what, father?'

'Everything...sorry for everything, son,' he muttered, and fell into a pain-wracked sleep.

When he awoke, nearly two hours later, it was to find himself encased in a sleeping-bag. He would never know the effort it had taken his son to manoeuvre it up his body, as he tried desperately not to touch the broken leg.

'How do you feel, dad...er, father?'

'I'll make a deal,' the man croaked up at him. 'If you give me a drink of water you can call me whatever you like.'

'It's a deal, dad,' he grinned, and reached for the bottle.

'How's the leg?' he asked a bit later. 'Does it hurt very much?'

'Not now, it feels numb. I think its the shock set in. Tell me, Michael, why did you run away? Did we treat you so badly?'

The boy shook his head. 'I wasn't running away, not really. I just wanted to see the Drakensberg. I've read everything about it, and I know the names of almost every climb. I'm sorry if you and mother were worried, but I would have come home once we'd reached Kqwedi's village.'

'Kqwedi?'

'That's Joseph's real name, dad. He's not from *kwaZulu*, he's Amangwane, and he's going home to die among his people. They live up past Cathedral Peak and that's where we were making for. Didn't you know where he came from?'

His father shook his head. 'It seems there are a lot of things I didn't know, or didn't want to. It takes a bit of pain, or a closeness with death, to make the grey cells work a bit clearer. Why don't you tell me about your journey?'

Michael rested his back against the cliff, legs dangling over the edge of the narrow, uneven ledge, and he talked. For once his father, his head lying on his son's lap, was an attentive listener.

He told of his decision to go with Joseph on his trek, and why the old man was doing it. He spoke of his own love of climbing, how he wanted to see the mountains close up, and imagine the great climbs that were there. Climbs that one day he too hoped to conquer. Of how only on the sheer face of a cliff, or climbing wall, did he feel complete in himself. His own master.

He told of the two families they'd met, and how different they were, yet how alike in their adversity. And the generosity they'd shown with the little they had, sharing it without thought or regret.

Michael spoke also of the old man's skill in hunting and his knowledge of the bush, despite his years of being a white man's lackey, and of the things he'd taught him.

When he spoke of the stories the old man had told, and the few tales he'd remembered in return, his father insisted he repeat them for his benefit. He was surprised at how much he could recall of their evenings together around the campfire.

His father would doze at times, and he would keep quiet and let him lapse into a painless unconsciousness. When he awoke, the boy would continue.

Once his father reached a hand up and held his wrist in a surprisingly strong grip. 'You don't stutter any more, Michael. I think that's a good sign, and I want to tell you something. I know I've been very harsh about this climbing business, but I did have my reasons. I want you to know that.'

'Its okay, dad,' the boy said softly. 'Try to get some rest.'

'No, I want to tell you this. You know that I have a brother, Uncle David in Eshowe. Well, once we had another brother. Your Uncle Michael, after whom you were named.'

He began to cough and Michael held the waterbottle to his lips. 'He was also a climber, and so was I. We put up some climbs in these mountains the two of us, but Michael, though he was five years younger, was by far the better climber. I was leading on the Sentinel, first climbed in 1910 and still a hard climb today, despite all the fancy stuff we use.'

He coughed again and Michael leaned forward with the bottle, but his father shook his head.

'To this day I don't know what happened. Michael was good, but had a tendency to cut corners for the sake of a higher hold, a chance of making a pitch, of scaling a new climb. Why he'd take a risk on a climb that went into the record books eighty years before I don't know, but I DO know I've blamed myself every single day since.'

He lapsed into silence and his son said nothing, simply holding him around the shoulders. He gazed out at the starless void of the cloudy night that had crept in on them.

'He fell, Michael. He fell, and there was nothing I could do to prevent it. They said he unclipped so that he could lunge around a boulder, that the rope would have been a restriction, but I find it hard to believe that he'd do such a thing. A moment of madness, perhaps. Who knows? But I've always blamed myself. And I never climbed again.'

Michael continued to gaze out at nothing. Nothing was better than the images conjuring up in his mind.

'When you said you wanted to climb, I felt sick. I didn't want the same thing happening to you, but I was wrong. You'll climb no matter what I say, for it's in your blood now. Just as it was in your uncle's, and mine too until the accident.'

They lapsed into silence then, and no words passed between them for a long while. The injured man asked for more water then passed into sleep again. Michael dozed fitfully but the cold and the noises of the night creatures below ensured that it was not for long.

He clung to his father as if he'd forgotten the belay that held him to the cliff, and only his own strength could keep him safe on the narrow ledge.

Near dawn his father woke and said he was hungry. Michael cut strips of *oribi* flesh and they both chewed on it.

They talked quietly of many things, some irrelevant, some of importance in their new acceptance of each other. At one time his father seemed delirious and he began to talk to himself in a low voice. Concerned, Michael wet his handkerchief with some of their precious water and mopped his brow.

'When I was a youngster, climbing these hills as often as I could, I used to know an old man who lived not far from here,'

His father smiled up at him, and to the boy's relief his speech was lucid again. 'He told me a remarkable story of when he fought in the Second World War, many miles from here, but it had its conclusion in the Drakensberg'

'I'd like to hear that story, dad,' Michael said softly, squeezing what moisture he could onto his father's forehead. Soon the sun would rise to their front, and they would have to bear its full power in their unprotected position.

Already, despite the hour, they could feel the heat.

Michael eased the sleeping bag down his father's body leaving it only as covering for the cruel injury to his leg. Their water was almost gone, and by noon they would be in trouble. If help didn't arrive by then.

'Hurry, Kqwedi, my friend,' the boy muttered under his breath. 'Please hurry.'

'What was that? Did you say something, Michael?'

His son shook his head, and smiled down at him. 'Only a prayer, dad. To Kqwedi. He won't let us down.'

'I'm sure he won't, my boy, I'm sure he won't,' and he closed his eyes against the brightness of the rising sun.

The boy lay back against the still-cool rock, as his father's weak, yet mellifluous, voice began to recite the story of a tree. No matter what happened now, Michael knew that something positive had come from near tragedy.

He and his father had become friends, and for that he would always be grateful.

CHAPTER SIXTEEN

THE GELIB TREE

Following the East African Force invasion of Italian Somaliland in 1941, the 1st Royal Natal Carbineers were approaching the village of Gelib. By a sheer coincidence of geography it turned out to be of strategic value to the war in North Africa, for it boasted both a road junction and a river crossing.

On the 22 February, a patrol of platoon strength, plus a mortar section, was sent out to intercept an enemy force that was retreating northwards up the Juba River. They moved through typical bush country, flat grassland interspersed with the occasional thick thorn.

From the edge of a once cultivated field, which had the dry stalks of an old cotton crop still standing, the patrol saw a band of Askaris, about platoon strength, two to three hundred yards away. They were just emerging from the trees at the river's edge, and an Italian officer led the way accompanied by an Askari carrying a large white flag.

It was obvious that their intention was to surrender and the Carbineers reacted with a mixture of disappointment and relief. Three men, a lieutenant, a sergeant and a private, were sent forward to accept the surrender, which in retrospect was not such a good idea. Instead the enemy should have been ordered out onto the open ground.

The three South Africans moved forward about a hundred yards and demanded the enemy's arms, but the Italian officer seemed reluctant to hand them over.

A sudden burst of firing broke out from the left flank, where a large force of the enemy lay concealed. The three went to ground but the sergeant was hit and killed on the first volley.

The officer and the private returned fire for as long as they could until their position became untenable, then they crawled back to their own lines, where the private was found to be seriously wounded.

As the rest of the platoon advanced through the grass, the men on the left bore the brunt of the flanking fire from the Italian ambushers, and all but one were killed.

Later, when the action was over, the bodies of these men lay in a straight line, charred by the burning grass, and facing the enemy. The men in the centre were able to find some cover in the vegetation and folds in the ground, and fortunately for them the Italians were shooting high.

A private was sent to the mortar section to lay down fire support, and then on to the Brigade HQ for help. As a precaution, the captain in charge sent a lance-corporal after him to make sure that at least one of them got through.

Behind them the battle continued, with the mortar fire passing close over their heads to assist the beleaguered Carbineers, and the burning grass sparked by enemy grenades forming a welcome and protective smoke-screen.

The lieutenant who had survived the initial part of the treacherous attack mustered the survivors, including the mortarmen, who had fired their last bombs and now fought as riflemen. This group reformed and made an attempt to clear the bush on the left, but were pinned down again.

Ammunition was now running low and their main firepower, the usually reliable Brens, were jamming because of the sand and dust. The survivors were holding on desperately by the time help arrived in the form of the armoured cars, and the heavy machine-gun fire soon knocked the fight out of the enemy.

When they surrendered it was accepted as honourably as the first white flag had been presented dishonourably. The death toll for this piece of infamy was near to one hundred.

The Carbineers buried their dead, thirteen in all, then pursued the foe to the north with new resolve and determination; no quarter asked, nor given. Gelib fell later that same day, signalling the collapse of the Italian Juba River line.

One of the relieving troops, a Carbineer officer, had gazed with sorrow upon the bodies of his dead and wounded comrades. Almost absently he picked up a handful of seeds from an acacia tree and put them in his pocket.

Years later, on his farm in the Loteni Valley beneath the shadow of Giant's Castle, he planted them. Only one survived, as if in memory of the Carbineers who had died on that terrible day in Italian Somaliland. The day that will always be spoken of in hushed tones wherever brave men talk, and the monstrous actions of those Italian officers will be forever an indictment of dishonour.

Today the Gelib tree stands on Natal Parks Board land, to which the farm now belongs, but it is still respected as a living monument to a small band of gallant men. Surrounded by a stout fence to protect it from animals, the tree stands tall, with wide branches sweeping out over the Loteni.

Like the men it immortalises, the Gelib Tree has endured hard times. The metre wide bole has been split down the middle by wind and weather, but a stout metal strap is banded tightly around it, and strong chains keep the branches in place.

Like a wounded warrior it stands proud and mighty, not unlike those heroes who went to fight, and die, in a war that was not of their making. In a land that was not theirs.

Michael's father had a lawyer's voice, which had risen with the dramatic words, and he stopped suddenly and coughed harshly. Michael allowed a trickle of water to pass his lips.

'When my leg is better I'll take you to see it, son,' he murmured. 'It stands for so much that is passing from our world, of bravery and selflessness. Of goodness, and remembering fallen comrades.'

His son knew he was not referring to the men who had died in that long-ago war, but of someone closer to home. They fell into a companionable silence, and words were not required for the bonding that was occurring between them.

Michael's watch showed a quarter past ten, and he knew he must attempt the dangerous manoeuvre of reversing the climb. They had to have water, especially the injured man, who had said nothing since his story of the Gelib Tree.

He eased himself out from under his father, laying his head gently on the rucksack. Unclipping himself from the belay, he started to ease himself over the lip, feet searching desperately for a toehold.

'Has it taken all this time for you to only just get there, *jong*?' the voice carried from below

He turned his head with difficulty and looked down. The grin that split his face was followed quickly by his scramble back onto the ledge.

Matching his grin was the old warrior. Standing next to him, the rope coiled around his shoulders, was the tall figure of Theo Thompson.

'This is your game, young man,' the farmer called up. 'What do you want us to do?'

'Get up above us, and find a good tree or rock to turn the rope around,' the boy ordered. 'Then drop the end down, and I'll tie it onto my father. You can lower him down to the bottom, but you'll have to double the rope as it looks a bit thin.'

'Right you are, Michael. We're coming up,' and the two men disappeared around the bottom of the cliff.

The boy clipped onto the belay again, and in a relatively short time he heard a shout from above. This was followed by the rope, which despite being lowered slowly was still accompanied by a few small stones.

He slipped the doubled rope under his father's armpits and tied a bowline tight against his chest. When the men above were ready he unclipped his father's belay.

'Dad, I'm going to tie the top of the sleeping bag around your waist,' he explained. 'It will act as a buffer if you bang your legs against the cliff.'

His father gave a weak smile. 'Okay, Michael, I'll try and use my hands to ward off. In case the other leg feels left out and tries to break itself as well.'

It was slow work. The boy kept his belay on and leaned out over the lip to push the rope away as it went past.

He winced each time he heard gasps of pain from below, and he ignored the occasional calls from above. Finally the rope went slack, and he leaned right out to see the injured man lying on the ground below the cliff.

'He's down,' he called up. 'Tie the rope off and I'll abseil.'

He took the longest of the tape slings and held it around his waist, then dropped a loop and pulled it up between his legs, securing the three loops with a karabiner. Next he took a *descendeur* from his rucksack. This was a small metal object shaped like a figure of eight, and he threaded a bight of the rope through the larger hole, passing it around the narrow neck or shank. The smaller hole clipped to the karabiner and he was ready for the descent.

He called out and received confirmation from aloft, then stepped out into space. His right hand held the controlling rope, the end that went below him, and he was able to regulate the speed of descent. He kept his left hand above the descendeur for stability, and took care not to touch the cliff and cause loose debris to fall onto his father.

He was soon down, and when he'd unclipped from the rope he stepped back and waved to the two figures at the cliff-head. They'd left two full waterbottles at the bottom, and he uncapped one and gave it to his father. The other he drank from greedily, and by the time Kqwedi and Theo joined them, both bottles were empty.

The tall farmer was carrying a pack.

'Found this at the top,' he said, then addressed the man on the ground. 'I assume it belongs to you.'

Michael's father nodded gratefully. 'I did plan to spend the night out here, though not quite the way it turned out.'

They all laughed, then Michael went into his planning mode again. 'We can use the rope and some straight branches to make a stretcher,' he said, beginning to enjoy the opportunity to show off his knowledge. 'Then we can carry him to...'

'Whoa,' the injured man held up a hand. 'You don't have to carry me anywhere. The chopper will be back to fetch me the day after tomorrow. They'll be expecting me to be a bit further north, but you can make some sort of mark on the ground to attract their attention.'

'A big H,' Michael said, with a smug expression, 'Is the correct one.'

'That will be fine. Now, if you'll just pass my pack over, and sit me upright, I'll make a brew. None of this roughing it nonsense, I've brought a gas stove with me.'

They propped his back against a rock, and used a groundsheet from his pack to provide shade above, then left him while they went to make the helicopter recognition sign. First they cleared a large circle of low bush and stones for the LZ, then used broken branches to gouge out a big H in the soft earth.

They paused once for a ten-minute tea break, then carried on, completing it just before noon. The rest of the meat, along with food his father had brought, provided them with a good meal.

After lunch Theo Thompson said he'd be taking his leave of them to get back to his family.

He shook hands all round, and as he bent over the injured man he found his hand gripped tightly.

'I've been doing some thinking,' Michael's father said, and the tone of his voice made them all look at him. His head was lying back against the rock, and he was staring up at the cliff that had so very nearly been the cause of his death.

'Mr Thompson, my son told me about your bad luck, and the poor treatment the bank gave you. I have a brother with a sugar-cane farm in Zululand. It's at Eshowe, and I know he's been looking for the right man to take over the running of it, so he can spend more time with another business he has. I think you could be the man he's looking for. IF you're interested, that is.'

'IF I'm interested...you're not having me on, are you, man? That would be a cruel thing to do.'

'No, I'm not having you on, Mr Thompson,' he smiled. 'And I'll prove it to you when the chopper gets here. You'll come with me in it, you and your family, and we'll go on to Empangeni. I'll phone my brother from there and he can pick us all up after they've put my leg in a cast. I'll make the most of my convalescence to spend some time with David and his family.'

'What about mum and the girls?' Michael asked, confused at his father's new attitude. For a couple of years now he'd been turning down invitations from Uncle David. 'Haven't got the time,' he would always say.

'They can drive up and join us.'

'And me?'

His father's new-found tolerance caused him to smile benignly at his son. 'You? You have a journey to finish, Michael. At the end of which you will help to get Jos...Kqwedi's home ready. A *rondavel* in his own *kraal,* and a few cows to make him a man of substance. In the land of the Amangwane though, not north in *kwaZulu.* I think you have many good years left in you, old man.'

The grizzled head dipped politely, and although he said nothing, Michael could tell his friend was well pleased.

'We'll pick you up in three weeks time, Michael, and on the way back we'll call in on your other friends. I'm sure we can help them also. Now, while Theo's collecting his family, how about making another brew, young man.'

The boy launched himself across the clearing and threw his arms around his father's neck.

'I drew my savings out,' he said in a low voice. 'Can you get me a new pipe and a pair of glasses for Kqwedi?'

'Of course,' his father smiled. 'But not with your money. I was the one who wouldn't listen, and now it looks like I've lost a good man. But perhaps I've found something else instead. An equally good son.'

CHAPTER SEVENTEEN

'How about telling us one of your stories, Joseph?' the white man asked, some time later, as they sat drinking their tea. 'Michael tells me you're the best teller of tales in all of Africa.'

'If that is so,' the old man smiled, no longer trying to hide his knowledge of the English language. 'Then he is surely a close second, for he too can weave a good tale. A short, sad story of intolerance comes to mind. It happened to a man I met in the barbers in Durban, who had been living in Cape Town. He was Xhosa, but he had many Zulu qualities that made him worth talking with.'

He produced his battered old corncob pipe and gravely began to fill it, as the boy suppressed a smile at the old man's condescending words...

TYPICAL

Walter Mnguni was feeling good. He had been part of the huge peace meeting on Grand Parade. His cheeks were still wet with tears as he thought of it, and there was a feeling of joy in his heart.

The Parade had been packed with people of many colours, there for one purpose only. To proclaim their desire, like the many posters held aloft, for 'Peace in our Land'.

White businessmen in collars and ties joined hands with black workers in blue overalls. Cape Muslims in hats and robes clung fervently to black taxi-drivers, and uniformed children from expensive schools linked arms with urchins. Street beggars, Whites as well as Blacks in the new South Africa, for once asked nothing but peace for all.

Religious groups and atheists stood next to each other and prayed for peace, each in their own way.

The inevitable speechmakers had their say from the steps of City Hall; party members who could not stop themselves adding political cant to their pleas for peace, 'Born-agains' drumming up trade for God and the next life if this one failed them, and City officials making the most of a chance to talk for once without castigation for the incompetent administration of their office.

The bus terminus on the edge of the Parade had long queues, so Walter was strolling past the Castle on his way to the harbour. There he would hitch along Marine Drive to Milnerton, and the squatter camp where he lived with his sister and her husband in the shack they had built. When Walter had arrived they simply built on a small room, from the materials left daily by passing vehicles or collected from rubbish dumps.

The squatting was illegal, for they were on council land, and the occupants for the most part were citizens of the independent homelands of Transkei and Ciskei. They preferred life in a squatter camp in South Africa to the bare existence of the homelands. Very little of the money and goods donated by SA found their way to the people it was intended for.

At first he found it hard to believe there were also white people living in the camp, for he'd always imagined that all Whites lived in big houses and drove expensive cars.

Life had been good for Walter Mnguni since he'd crossed the Ciskei border and moved down to the Cape. Having begun as a casual labourer in a builder's yard, he'd been given a regular job as a counter-man. His willingness to work, and the passable English he'd been taught in mission school, had been noticed.

He had also found himself a girl. Beauty Xaba, and she was indeed a beauty. Her good looks had found her a position in a dress shop in Cape Town. Walter adored her, and they were saving hard to buy a real house one day. In the meantime they might put together a shack of their own, for Walter could get off-cuts from his employer, and the local council, despite that they were illegal settlements, was going to provide water and toilet facilities to the camps.

The sun was beaming down on the little Xhosa as he wandered down Jan Smuts and past the Nico Malan Opera House. He looked at the building with affection, for when he'd first seen it he'd made a vow. One day he would go in there, dressed as well as any White, and he would pay for the best seats in the house. And he would take Beauty.

Another thing Walter had found in the Cape was religion.

His parents had been 'Bush Baptists', and each Sunday they would gather at a chosen spot. There they would sing hymns and pray, like the church he went to now, but then would begin the wailing and people crying out their sins before God, and the minister would beat them sorely and with vigour to drive out the Devil.

Walter had an aversion to being beaten sorely and with vigour, so he did not go back to the Bush Baptists once he was a grown man. But he loved the Bible, especially the parables. His favourite was the Good Samaritan, and he knew many people were Samaritans, regardless of their colour. He too would like to be one, some day.

His chance came sooner than expected, for as he came to the front of the Opera House he saw a man lying on the grass. As he watched, the man rolled over and climbed painfully to his knees.

He was a White and his face was covered in blood. He suddenly collapsed again.

Walter looked around. There were other people passing through the gardens but they ignored the injured man, either assuming he was drunk or deciding it was none of their business.

Well it was HIS business, Walter decided. It was obvious the poor man had been robbed, and he needed taking care of. It was the only Christian thing to do, and wasn't he a Christian after all?

He bent down and rolled the man over onto his back, and was just loosening his tie when a Police van pulled up in front of the gardens.

To Walter's astonishment, the two constables jumped on him.

Assuming it was the Black robbing the White on the ground, they threw him down on his face and handcuffed him, then they bundled him into the back of the van.

While they waited for an ambulance, people began to gather and peer in at the arrested man. The yellow Police van was a small pick-up with a solid canopy, and wire covered the windows at the back instead of glass.

Walter was shamed and mortified by the nasty looks and threatening remarks, and he sighed with relief when the van finally pulled away.

When they arrived at the Police station the worst part began. He was taken to an interview room, where the arresting officers shouted questions at him and slapped him around when he wouldn't answer them. Not that Walter wasn't willing to answer their questions, he simply could not understand their guttural Afrikaans.

'Please,' he begged finally, after he'd received a particularly stinging smack in the ear. 'I do not understand the Holland tongue. Can you please speak English?'

This made the policemen howl with laughter.

'Can we speak English?' one roared. 'Of course we can speak English, you stupid *kaffir*.'

'What did you do with the stolen property?' the other demanded. 'The man's wallet, watch and I.D. book were missing. Did you have a mate with you, eh?'

'P...please, sir, I did not r...rob the p...person,' Walter stammered. 'I w...went to help h...him. Ask him, p...please.'

'Oh, we will, man,' the big one said. 'When he wakes up.'

Walter was stripped of his belongings; even his belt and tie, and his shoelaces. What did they think he was going to do with them? Use them to escape?

He was shoved into a large holding cell that had three other occupants, two Cape Coloureds and a fellow Black. All were drunk, and spent their time smoking, snoring loudly in drunken slumber, or using the single toilet to relieve themselves or vomit into. Walter, who didn't drink or smoke, felt nauseous, and had never been more miserable in his life.

Several hours passed before the two constables came and took him from the cell. At the watch-house he was given back his belongings and told he could go. He received no apology or explanation.

Only by chance, as he was threading his shoelaces, did he hear one of the officers' say in disgust, 'I thought it was too easy, now we've got to find the two Coloured buggers who did it.'

Walter, shaken by his experience, managed to get home in one of the hundreds of crowded kombis known as 'Kafir Taxis'. He felt so ashamed that he mentioned his experience to no one.

And life went on.

About a month later, Walter had been to a late night church meeting, and was making his way to the terminus to get the last bus home. As he was about to cross Adderley Street, he heard a sound coming from a doorway behind him. He turned and saw a white man lying with his back against the door. His face was a mess, with blood pouring freely from open wounds. His nose was broken.

The occasional passers-by hurried on, afraid to become involved.

'Please, help me,' the man mumbled through smashed lips.

'They were breaking in...I tried to...stop them. I'm a... Police officer.'

Walter's look of pity changed to shock as he recognised the wretched man as the larger of the two constables who had locked him up.

He desperately wanted to be a Samaritan but he was also frightened of the Police now. Perhaps they would blame him for this also.

So Walter Mnguni put compassion to one side and scurried across the road for his bus.

It was quite a while before a Police vehicle arrived on the scene and found their colleague, unconscious.

'There were people going past,' he told them later. 'But nobody stopped. Except a black oke who looked, but didn't help.'

'Typical of a Black,' one of his mates replied. 'Wouldn't cross the street to help their own mother. Bloody typical.'

Michael looked from one to the other, as his father laughed aloud and the old man sniggered quietly.

'Was that a true story?' he demanded, which made his father laugh all the more.

'All stories are true eventually,' Kqwedi said evasively.

'It is now your turn, *jong*.'

'Perhaps I can tell one,' the injured man offered. 'With a similar theme to yours. It also involves the Police, and their habit of jumping to conclusions where black people are concerned...'

MYANI I TAS

The outskirts of the township were poorly lit and only the weak rays of a three-quarter moon shed light on the landscape.

A Police vehicle came slowly along the road. It was a long-wheel based Landrover, wire grills over the windows as much to restrain the prisoners inside as for protection from outside.

A grey figure was hurrying along the side of the road, and the lights of the oncoming vehicle showed him to be casually but neatly dressed. He was carrying a small brown case.

The Police rover veered and came to a halt just in front of the man, causing him to stop suddenly. Nobody left the vehicle at first, and the only movement was the nervous shuffling of the lone black man.

Doors opened and two uniformed men confronted the pedestrian.

'*Wat maak jy hier, kaffir?*' The white sergeant barked. 'What are you doing here?'

The man stepped closer into the lights of the Landrover. He was tall for a Zulu, and wore spectacles.

'I...am sorry,' he said in good English. 'I do not speak Afrikaans.'

The spokesman nodded to his fellow officer.

'*Vra hom*,' he ordered. 'Ask him.'

The black constable moved closer to the man with the case.

He spoke rapidly in Zulu and again the other man shook his head.

'I'm sorry,' he apologised once more. 'I...have been away too long. I've nearly forgotten my own language.'

'You keep saying you're sorry, boy,' the sergeant snapped in heavily accented English. 'What the Hell are you so sorry for, eh?'

A thick pale finger prodded the black man in the chest. It reminded him of the fat grubs that live beneath logs in the bush.

'Nothing,' he said quickly, hating himself for his fear, hating the ones who caused it even more.

'Nothing isn't good enough, *kaffir*,' the white man persisted. 'What's that you're carrying?'

'It's...just a case,' he stammered.

'We can see that. Open it,' came the order.

'I do not have the key,' the black man lied, though why he didn't know.

'Never mind,' the sergeant said. 'We'll look at it on the way to the station. Put him in the back.'

Ignoring the weak protests of his fellow Black, the second Policeman grabbed him roughly by the arm and bundled him into the back of the waiting vehicle.

He secured the doors from the outside then took his place behind the wheel.

As they drove slowly along the road, the officer in the passenger seat placed the case carefully on his knees. He turned and looked at the man in the back, separated by the thick mesh.

'What's your name, boy?'

'John,' came the hesitant reply. 'John Mbeki.'

'Well, John Mbeki,' the Policeman grinned. 'Let us see what a rooster like you is doing with such a nice leather case as this. Old, but nice. Someone's taken very good care of it.'

He produced a pocketknife and tried to force it into the lock.

'What might we have here?' he mused as he worked to open it.

'Some ammunition maybe, or even a pistol. Are you a jewel thief perhaps, John Mbeki?'

He nudged the driver and pointed the knife at the case.

'Miskien is hy 'n wild dief,' perhaps he is a poacher, he laughed. *'Miskien is daar 'n bok in die tas.'* Perhaps he is hiding a buck in the case.

The black driver laughed uproariously at the thought of a large buck hidden in the small case.

They were both still laughing as the Landrover went over the mine.

The force of the explosion drove upwards beneath the engine and the vehicle flew backwards in a huge arc. It landed with its wheels in the air, all four still spinning.

After the noise of the blast the ensuing silence was absolute, and John Mbeki shook his head and tried to orientate himself.

He heard a groan from close by and memory came flooding back to him, the faint light through the wire mesh being enough to give him his bearings.

He managed to turn so his feet were facing in the direction of the rear doors and he kicked wildly at them. A pain shot up his right leg from the knee, but in their weakened state the doors gave on that first kick.

He tumbled out onto the dirt road and dragged himself upright by holding on to the rover. He gingerly felt over his body, but apart from minor cuts and bruises only the knee seemed to have lasting damage.

Glancing at the upturned vehicle he thought incongruously that it resembled a giant dung beetle, which having fallen off its ball was struggling to right itself.

He stumbled round to the driver's side and wrenched open the door. Once glance at the angle of the man's neck and he knew help was unnecessary. The shard of glass protruding obscenely from his left eye confirmed this.

He limped round to the far side and found the door had been ripped off with the impact.

The Policeman in the passenger seat lay half out of the cab, and he groaned again as John Mbeki reached across him.

He began to withdraw the case when a weak hand clamped down on his wrist.

'Looking for your gun, eh, *kaffir*? So you can finish the job your *Gott vor domp* friends have started.'

The effort of talking made him break into a coughing fit, and the black man slowly prised the fingers from his arm.

He took the case, laid it on the ground by the vehicle, and extracted a small key from his pocket. As he opened it he felt the stricken man's eyes upon him, glaring hotly through a mask of blood pouring from a head wound.

His face held a look of perverse satisfaction as he sank into merciful unconsciousness.

It was with some surprise, therefore, that he awoke to find himself propped against the bank at the side of the road, and he felt the bandage around his head and saw his left arm and leg secured in makeshift splints.

A tourniquet bound his arm tightly above the splint.

John Mbeki was bending over him, and as he straightened, moonlight glinted on the needle in his hand.

A feeling of euphoria passed over him as the morphine took effect and he could no longer feel pain.

The tall black man placed the needle in his case, closed it carefully and stood up. One of the lenses was cracked on his spectacles, the web-like pattern giving him a strangely comical aspect.

'Your radio was still operable,' he looked down at the injured man. 'Help will be here soon.'

He turned to go, case in hand.

'I...want to thank...you...Mr Mbeki,' the effort to say the words did not come from his wounds alone.

The black man looked back and smiled sadly.

'It is Doctor Mbeki, actually,' he said, and limped off down the dusty road.

Back to his original destination, the small house on the edge of the township. From where he had left for England, and his medical scholarship, so many years before.

And his grip on his *myani I tas* - the small case - was as firm as the day his parents had given it to him, for he was aware of the sacrifices they had made to buy it.

'I told you that sometimes things are not as they would appear to be, Michael' Joseph said with a smile, and the boy smiled back with a vigorous nod of his head.

CHAPTER EIGHTEEN

When night finally crept upon them, they were ready for it.

Their bivouac was made, a fire blazed, and there was ample wood to last until morning. The old hunter's bow had provided two fat guinea fowl, and they were plucked ready for roasting on the fire.

When the boy went to bed that night, it was with a full stomach and an even fuller heart, for he was lying between his father and his best friend, beneath the towering peaks of his beloved Drakensberg.

He slept that deep, dreamless sleep that only happens to the very young - or the very old.

Late the next day the family walked into the camp. The boy, fully recovered now, rode high on his father's shoulders, and little Dolly skipped and danced around her mother as though she'd just come from a friend's house a few doors away.

Marie Thompson could not hide her delight about the job her husband had been offered, and she fussed around Michael's father as though he was royalty. She took over the cooking, and this time Kqwedi's bow had placed plump wood pigeons on the menu.

The camp was subdued that evening, for on the following day the helicopter would arrive, and they would split up. However, once Theo Thompson produced the last of the Klipdrift, and the injured man a flask of whisky from his pack, the conversation livened up. Mrs Thompson allowed herself a few sips, and even Michael had a drop of watered down whisky.

More stories were told that night, but the one that stayed in the boy's mind the longest was one related by the woman. For he was sure THAT was the truth...

GREEN MEALIES

The two women sat on the back *stoep* and howled with laughter.

They were carried away to the heights of mirth, snorting with a maniacal glee that had its origins in something as mundane as the denim shirt that hung on the line.

They chattered in conversational Zulu, an unknown quantity to most Whites, who usually spoke only 'kitchen Zulu' to give instructions to their staff, and were unaware of the richness of the language.

They merely heard the Blacks 'jabbering away'; in what some ignorant Whites would call their 'monkey talk'. The ability to discuss at great length a simple subject, some object of no consequence, was a gift in itself.

Socrates and his fellow Athenians had that gift. Few civilisations since then have spared the time, or perhaps had the patience, to philosophise over a subject with very little form.

It has been left to the generals to talk of war and the past, the ecologists to discuss the environment and the future, and the politicians to worry about the present on a global scale.

Zulus keep their discussions to a piece of paper blowing past, the shape of a tree in the distance...or in the present instance, a shirt hanging on the line.

'It is *isomi* - blue,' insisted the fat one, giggling still after the obscene illustration the other had made to the way the shirttail had been flapping in the small breeze.

'*Ngwevu* - grey,' laughed the thinner woman.

'*Mina cabanga kumbe yona ai washila lungileyo* - I think maybe it is not washed right,' cried the large one.

'Well, Violet, you do the washing around here,' the other said, laughing uproariously.

I listened to their voices rising up to the open window of my bedroom, where I was painting them both. Unbeknown to them of course. My easel was set up by the window, and I would occasionally steal a look down at them.

They were like children, totally uncomplicated, and something in me wanted to preserve them the way they were now. In the same way that we want to keep our children the same for ever, never wanting them to change - or to grow up and away from us.

In some perverse way I suppose we want to remain there ourselves, in the land of 'now'.

Sitting on the back *stoep*, happy with each other and their simple, but clever, conversation. Captured for all time on my canvas.

Violet came from Durban, and the other woman, Elsie, from Northern Natal, which consisted mostly of Afrikaner farms and homesteads. She had been brought up on an Afrikaner farm, though not one of the bigger ones. A *dorp* she would call it, for her Afrikaans was as good as her Zulu, though her English was heavy with accent.

As a child, she told me, they were very poor. She was embarrassed that most of her Zulu friends had shoes, whereas she would go barefoot.

I watched the fat one, my cook, go off to her kitchen. I called it her kitchen because I was not welcome there, and allowed in only under sufferance. My husband was not allowed in at all. It was Violet's domain.

She returned in a little while bearing a steaming bowl of green mealies, generously smeared with butter, and they both fell to with a will.

Mealies are corn on the cob, and I can never understand why the British and Americans eat the plastic yellow variety, when the 'green' ones out here are so much nicer.

With mouths full of mealie, the two middle-aged women were still chattering away, spraying each other liberally and laughing fit to burst.

This was something other than I had originally depicted them, huddled together and nudging each other to emphasise a point. This was more spontaneous, more evocative of the feel of Africa.

I changed canvases quickly and sketched furiously to capture them while they were still in full flow, hands holding mealies flying around in graphic point making, and the air around them alive with words and merriment.

I still have that picture. It hangs in my sister's house and soon, when we have a roof over our heads once more, I'm going to take it back and hang it in the most prominent place. It won first prize in the main Durban art competition, but that's not why I'm so proud of it.

No, it's because it reminds me of my past, my 'roots' to coin an over-used word, and I modestly admit I did capture the spirit of the time quite well.

The shiny black face of Violet the cook, and the careworn loving features of my Afrikaner mother, God rest her.

Until the day she died she worried about fitting in to her daughter's household, the daughter who had a big farm and could afford a cook and a housemaid. Never before in her life had she lived in a house with servants, and she had been embarrassed. As when she was a child, and did not have shoes when the black children did.

But after a while she found her own way of fitting in, as my canvas had captured. Fitting in so well, in fact, that she was even allowed in the kitchen, a singular honour indeed, and was even showing Violet some of those wonderful old Afrikaner recipes.

I wonder if she knew I was as proud of her as she ever was of me.

I hope so.

The old man and the boy, both clad in the garb of warriors of the Ngwane, stopped on the path that led into the village.

Beyond the village, the waters of the Umlambonja raced down from Cathedral Peak, gathering the numerous cold mountain streams. Pools reflected the beautiful grass beehives dotting the hillsides, and the surrounding mealie lands created a patchwork pattern.

The scene was unique, giving the impression that time had stood still since the mid-nineteenth century, for it was then that the Amangwane had returned to their old home in the shadow of *uKhahlamba*, following a life of war, pillage, starvation, migration, fragmentation, and the murder of their chief, Matiwane.

Shouts from the herdboys tending the cattle and goats were almost hushed by the noise from the fast-flowing rivers, as they rushed by through the valleys and ravines.

A group of people had come out to meet them, and in the forefront was a man who was the mirror image of the old visitor, but younger by some twenty years.

'I am Kqwedi, once of this village,' the words of his native tongue suddenly felt strange after so many years speaking the language of the English. 'I have come home.'

'I am also called Kqwedi, after my father,' the other man said. 'You have many grandchildren here, and you are welcome at our fire, father. As is your friend.'

The formalities over, they fell into each other's arms, the old man and he of middle years who had not seen his father since he was but three years old.

When they finally broke from their embrace, a sea of people surrounded the old man; his grandchildren, great-grandchildren, and some of these had children of their own. At least he would not be lonely in his remaining years, Michael thought.

He followed happily towards the grass beehives of the village. He had more than two weeks in this place, and he would use the time well.

His friend Kqwedi would see to that, before the hillsides would ring with cries of 'Hamba kahle' - 'go carefully' - as he returned to his home in the city.

A changed home now, thanks to the man he'd once known as Joseph. The man who had brought him to the Dragon Mountains.

His Place of Whispers.

ends.................

Lightning Source UK Ltd.
Milton Keynes UK
UKOW051039211111

182418UK00001B/8/P